# Fi̲

## to a Change of Mind

# Prelude
## to a Change of Mind

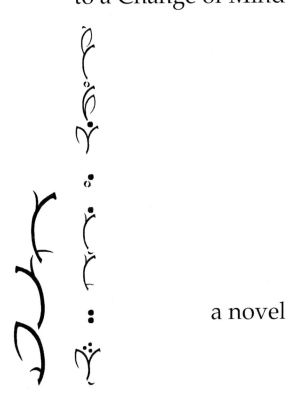

a novel

## by Robert Stikmanz

Second Edition
The First Book in *The Lands of Nod*

Dalton
Publishing
AUSTIN, TEXAS

Dalton Publishing
P.O. Box 242
Austin, Texas 78767
*daltonpublishing.com*

Printed in the United States of America

Second edition, 2007
The first edition of this work was published by the author
from 2000 to 2006 via the print-on-demand publishing service,
Xlibris.

Edited by Ric Williams

Cover Design & Typography by Robert Stikmanz
Cover Illustration by Stikmanz

ISBN-10: 0-9740703-5-X
ISBN-13: 978-0-9740703-6-0
LCCN: 2007920122

This is a work of fiction. Any resemblance to actual persons
living or dead is coincidence, except of course in the instance
of those small, non-human individuals who have colonized
the author's mind through acts of psychic hegemonization. No
coincidence in that.

ATTENTION ORGANIZATIONS AND SCHOOLS:

Quantity discounts are available on bulk purchases of this book
for educational purposes or fund raising.

For information, contact Dalton Publishing via email at: *deltina@
daltonpublishing.com*.

Dedicated to the late Ricardo Sánchez,
an intuit in the grand style

# Acknowledgments

WERE IT NOT FOR THE FRIENDSHIP, encouragement and example of many, this book either would not have been conceived or would be vastly different. The world in which this account is set was discovered in 1984—in the context of another book still in development—at a time when I was collaborating in business, art, politics, music, and publishing with Michael Ambrose. As influences on *Prelude to a Change of Mind*, Mike and his science fiction/weird fiction/fantasy journal, *The Argonaut*, must be rated huge.

Other writers, publishers, and particular works to whom or which I owe an incalculable debt include:

Ed Buffaloe, editor/publisher of *Aileron* and poet of *The Nolan's Ghost* and *Xlate;*

Michael Gilmore, co-editor of *Aileron* and poet of *Lyrika* and *Celtica;*

the late Ricardo Sánchez, for all his poetry but especially in this circumstance for his prose work, *Bertrand and the Mehkqoverse: a Xicano Filmic Nuance;*

Mark Smith, author of *Riddle;*

Pat LittleDog as oral historian of *Border Healing Woman*, author of *Afoot in a Field of Men*, and poet of *Tonics, Teas, Roots & Remedies;*

and the late Albert Huffstickler, poet of (among others) *Night Diner, Walking Wounded, The Old Man,* and *The Smell of Distance.*

To my enormous benefit, six very special readers provided detailed responses to early drafts. First among these is James Rossignol, who read, reread, and reread again with intelligence, candor, patience, and generosity. Those same terms apply to the thoughtful reactions of Ed Buffaloe, Jerry Lincecum, Carla Webb Maywald, Sandra Westergren, and the late Joanie Whitebird.

For extraordinary support and encouragement I owe thanks to Rick Adams, Carolyn Brittin, Jane Focht-Hansen, Jim Harris, Don Lewis, Mark Lewis, the late Rose Lewis, Tony Manuel,

Cleveland Maxwell, Linda Nelson, Karen Pittman, Nancy Salay, Mary Saunders, Mary Shepherd, and Pace Smith.

You would not hold this volume were it not for the commitment and hard work of my editor, Ric Williams, and publisher, Deltina Hay. May blessings and bounty shower them both.

Lastly and most inclusively, la compañera de mi vida, Janel Nye, reads all with fresh eyes, never stints opinion or advice, and challenges every hurdle with the spirit of possibility. To her, besos, abrazos, and muchísimas gracias.

Robert Stikmanz
Austin, Texas

## *Editor's Note*

As assiduous as I am in my pursuit of the elimination of error as old Diogenes for the glow of an ideal truth, I am reminded by the wrr of a wandering thrm that mystery is no error & flaws are but a frame for brilliance; that nothing is truly lost nor sorrow a diminishment of transcendent beauty. Thus, dear reader, Master Stikmanz, in his linguistically studied & peripatetically slipper'd ginger way, assured me that the sundry variations & capitalizations of all the creatures of the Noddish world, and I use that term most loosely as Nod is but the name of the game, nay, the holy oracle, by which certain devotees of the co-existent universe, and that too is a loose descriptor for the intersecting realities described in this first foray into said intersecting realities, one of which is this self-same world whereby you read these scribblings, speak of things as they are were & ever never will be, are exactly as they should be in this transconsensual moment. So rest easy, the thrm'm await to ease all pain. Just have a pipe with Jackanapes, crank up the zoot horn croons, & slip most sweetly into the true world of the brilliantly unreal. The editing has been done.

Ric Williams

# Foreword to a Prelude

THE WAIL OF A TENOR SAX, the thump of a bass, the gnashing of synth keyboards and guitars, the metronomic rhythm of a drum machine augmented by random whackings of old Ford hubcaps, cast-off electrical junction boxes and miscellaneous resounding found stuff uncorked and decanted in a wedge-shaped office tucked into the corner of a senescent strip mall at the savagely urban intersection of Interstate 35 and U.S. Highway 290 in what in 1984 was still northeast (as opposed to central) Austin. By day the space was a small, quiet, not-prosperous-enough commercial graphic arts enterprise adjacent to a busy franchise print shop; by night it transformed into an eerily lit studio production space seething with patch cords, speakers, tape recorders, and mix boards—the entire room mic'd so taut with reverberation that the mere twist of a bottle cap could become inspiration for another improvisational jam, length and direction unknown until it happened.

Other times, the studio served as meeting hall and newsletter production bullpen for the raggedy-ass Socialist Party of Texas, its torchbearer the anarchist urban gorilla Cleveland Maxwell, who provided the beer and—with Rob and other heads—plotted revolution. No small coincidence that the member rosters of SP-TX and Jam Cadre were nearly identical.

Such was part of the context in which the someday to be Robert Stikmanz, but then still just Rob Lewis, clacking away on a primitive word processor so obscurely named that it will likely never be curated in the Museum of Obsolete Tekker Knowledges, wrote the primordial draft of the story out of which came the novel you're about to read. In between sharing duties of our graphics studio and musical sessions of aforementioned loose-knit group of friends known as Jam Cadre, Rob would retreat to the dim inner office, a glass-enclosed room dominated by monolithic phototypesetting equipment, to huddle before his C/PM computer and tap away at the story.

In earlier times and places, Rob and I, some of the Cadres and other friends collaborated on sundry magazines, chapbooks, poetry readings, and arts events. The eye of the vortex was a thin sliver of the student-infested edge of the Hyde Park neighborhood just north of the UT-Austin campus. There, during the gathering night of the first Reagan term, neighbors and friends drifted in and out of each other's houses and lives, a few congenial spirits coming together for periods of time brief and long to collaborate on creative projects. Some souls went their own ways earlier or later, a few went into and out of business together, others into and out of closer relationships. It was a time of all-night chess games, spinning the platters, pick-up afternoon baseball in the neighborhood park, late-night poetry readings, wee-hour excursions to diners and cafes—and casting about for meaningful ways to resist or subvert the oppressively dominant paradigm.

Some of us were not just writers and poets: we wanted to be publishers. I'd been issuing the small-press SF/fantasy zine *Argonaut* since 1972. Along about 1982, I got together with Rob, Mark Smith, Rhandon Hurst, and a few other like-minded individuals to publish the literary popular-culture journal *Window Magazine*. At the same time, Ed Buffaloe and Michael Gilmore were producing their wonderful *Aileron,* still one of the finest literary zines ever to come out of central Texas. And over and around and above us all was poet Albert Huffstickler—"Huff"— the coffee-drinking, cigarette-smoking, free-spirited genius loci of the Austin literary scene, such as it was or has ever been.

Later, in actual commercial business together as Liberty Graphics, Rob and I produced a number of chapbooks for Huff, including the legendary *Night Diner* and the first incarnation of his multiform chapbook *The Old Man.* We also continued *Argonaut* and did other short-run print efforts as we found time and money. And, naturally, we discovered, like so many writers and artists before us possessed of a burning ambition to publish, that literary action and the pressures of running a small business rarely mixed in one's favor—but damn, it sure was nice to have our very own production studio and ready access to cheap printing!

But through it all, Rob kept writing.

In time, of course, Life Went On: the band dissolved, the business folded, and the friends followed separate ways. Around the end of 1988 Rob married and left for a period of exile in Iowa. I kept *Argonaut* going for a few more years, finally ending its two-decades-plus run in 1995. In the late 1990s Rob could no longer resist the call of Austin. He got unmarried and moved back. As he told me recently, he gave up "trying to write bad poetry" to engage his formidable talents in more interesting prose directions, the fruit of which you hold in your hands.

The foregoing contextual digression may not mean much to you unless you were a part of it or part of other times and places like it, but perhaps it reveals something about inspirations behind the present work. As may be inevitable in the case of a work born from a swelling mix of liberation politics, raucous noise, creative labor, and riotous fun, your ultimate interpretation of *Prelude to a Change of Mind* will differ from mine and everyone else's. Probably you have never before read anything quite like it. But stick around. I guarantee you will be hearing much more from the changing mind of Mr. Stikmanz.

Michael Ambrose
Editor & Publisher, Argo Press

# Prelude
## to a Change of Mind

*Between two worlds Life hovers like a star,*
  *'Twixt Night and Morn, upon the horizon's verge.*
*How little do we know that which we are!*
  *How less what we may be! The eternal surge*
*Of Time and Tide rolls on and bears afar*
  *Our bubbles; as the old burst, new emerge,*
*Lashed from the foam of ages; while the graves*
*Of Empires heave but like some passing waves.*

Lord Byron
*Don Juan*, 15: XCIX

# *One*

## ⟩

THE TINY WOMAN STEPPED FROM THIN air and darted off without a look to see who followed. In a burst of speed, she dropped to all fours, galloping across the cabin and through a door to a second room at the back. Her way was obstructed and her path confused by increasing dozens of her kind coming out of the air to fill the log walled structure. She zigged and zagged past diminutive women and men, old and young, materializing around her, complicating her run with the abrupt fact of themselves and the stout wooden rods most of them carried. A final leap carried her to the side of a flushed and thrashing form struggling on a low cot.

On the bed a human, a young woman—some might still have said girl—moaned and sweated in restless, fevered sleep. She muttered brokenly, crying out now and again for faces absent or mercies unknown. Her arms and legs knocked with great agitation but little force against the low wood frame that bore the thin, canvas-covered pad on which she tossed, its lattice of stretched hemp creaking loudly.

The bed was simple, the homemade mattress stuffed in small part with lumps of batting, and in larger part with scraps of old fabric too worn or ratted for other practical use. Modest though it was, it was nevertheless fitted with muslin sheets and wool blankets against chill nights.

At the head of the cot, against the wall above the sick girl's head, the tiny woman leaned forward, her dancing fingertips playing lightly over the flush of the girl's face. With coos and sighs, the slight figure warbled as she worked, and sang wordless lilting harmonies to the girl's moans. More of the little people moved close to the bed, singing wordlessly, contributing a palette of wrring and chuttering calls, stroking, patting, or tapping, so that no portion of the girl went untouched or unserenaded.

A steady stream of the arrivals moved in and out through the door, some staying to mill behind the first rank at the bed. These sang in concert with those who touched, ready to slip into an open place whenever one nearer the bedside moved away. Beyond the threshold, the outer chamber teemed with these beings, all barking or chirping or crooning a variegated racket. Periodic laughter rippled through the mass of small men and women stroking, patting and caressing each other a room away from the sick girl.

Constant at the bed, the tiny nurse nimbly worked the girl's forehead and temples in a light massage. The three fingers and two thumbs of each of her hands spread widely apart in a vast reach that allowed her to stroke a broad area with a simple motion. Like all her companions except the very youngest, she wore a skirt and shawl of sturdy homespun, unbleached, undyed, unadorned. The shawl was held by a simple clasp at the shoulder. Unlike most of the others, however, she carried no staff.

The faces of these small folk were bare, but their hair grew lushly in a thick mane that sprouted from scalp and jaw line, disappearing at the base of the neck into the tops of their shawls. A light fur was visible on the legs extending below their skirts and on the arms that reached from beneath their upper garments.

Through the twittering, chattering, lilting din bounding off the walls, an interference-ridden short-wave voice, or successive voices, barely rose to audibility from a radio in the main room. It pattered ceaselessly in a tinny, excited whisper, cataloging the passage back and forth of despoliation, murder and brutal fervors in the name of Il Duce, the Emperor, the Fuhrer, of Democracy and His Majesty. Through the crackle of the ether, it spoke of the Revolution, the Fatherland, the Motherland, the Republic, in the name of Freedom, of Destiny, of the Red Army, of God and Country, of Profit, on and on in tones all the more alarming for their dispassionate calm.

The room in which the young human tossed was a lean-to, an add-on intended perhaps as a large pantry, but now snugly filled with the cot, a chair and a large chest—and two to three dozen singing, barking, cooing, trilling, active, milling, beskirted beings of small stature and ceaseless activity. The low rear wall was about the same height as these folk, so they stood freely beneath the ceiling's angle even in the tight pass between wall and bed. One window pierced the end wall across from the foot of the cot, though the opening was tightly shuttered, and did little to relieve the chamber's gloom. Beneath this window stood the trunk and atop the trunk lay a brush and mirror. Apart from the plank door that opened out into the main room, nothing interrupted the bare, rough timbers of the walls except a hand-drawn calendar and a small shelf by the head of the bed that served for a nightstand. The bed itself was a simple wooden frame raised on stubby legs just enough to clear the ankle high boots placed underneath in company with a pair of well-worn loafers. Both pairs of shoes belonged to the delirious young woman struggling unconsciously within the sheets.

Her name was Meg, Patricia Margaret Christmas, to be precise, but for all her eighteen years she had been called and had called herself Meg. The cot she so restlessly occupied stood in her room, a tiny room, in the cabin she shared, in season, with her father. That season was the burn time, the hot days and dry weeks when forestlands are most vulnerable to fire. She and her father were part of a thin pepper, vigilant ones and twos, strewn through these woods to watch for the telltales of combustion.

This particular cabin, a rough but tight structure of heavy, clay caulked boles, stood in a high grassy clearing among mountain forest. The meadow opened in a mixed wood of fir and aspen, graced at its upper end by the addition of down wandering spruce, and gated where a path entered its lower edge by two ponderosa pines. Beside the cabin, its adjacent watchtower—though still a good, huffing climb below the tree line—stood eminent above a broad range of lesser slopes and changing timber. During their periods of residence, father and daughter shared this unassuming home, and shared also the task of peering from the tower, gazing out from their clearing over the expanse of lands falling away into storybook vistas, eyes open against signs of fire.

As Meg lay self-bound in her tangled cot, remnant fever still tossing her weakly now and again, the season was near its final days. Fall color was well advanced in the foliage over which she was charged to watch. Even an unfamiliar observer, scanning the site she and her father had occupied over the last months, could see that it was partially secured against imminent departure. First snow in that high place would isolate it completely.

Rewarding the persistent ministrations of the small folk were signs that the girl was resting easier. The fever held on, bated if not beaten, but she lay more quietly amidst the song erupting on all sides. Her lidded eyes danced in dream.

She mistook their voices for birdcalls. Dreaming, she floated in an enormous tropical colony of giant parakeet flamingos. She dreamed they nuzzled her, and some of them, not those close by, interrupted their otherwise unending polyphony with laughter.

The little beings who attended her were not long in perceiving a gradual relaxing of the crisis, and a quite evident note of relief entered their vocalizations. An old greyhair had stood at Meg's side, clasping the girl's hand and patting it tenderly all the long hours of the worst, while others more actively worked about her form. This oldster now lifted the hand against its cheek and released it, retiring to the far corner by the door to curl up and, without ceremony, go to sleep.

A young man, walnut skinned and ruddy maned except for a white patch in the hair under his chin, stepped into the open place at the bedside, dropped his staff at his feet, and took up Meg's hand. He yodeled expressively to the room at large, a cry that was picked up at the door by a mother with a prattling toddler on her hip, and passed by her with embellishments to the room beyond. There it was echoed, improvised on, adjusted to and adapted until a memory of its shape was part of every detail in that dense tapestry of sound.

The young man stroked, rubbed, tapped, and patted Meg's hand and upper arm, much as his companions were doing over the rest of her body. Much as the woman at the head of the bed did with Meg's face and crown. Some of those who attended the girl wore expressions of focused, diagnostic concentration. Others showed faces like that a virtuoso might wear while playing a favorite song on a cherished instrument. Those not at the immediate bedside expressed a more general exuberance, patting and brushing themselves and each other nearly as much as their companions did Meg. They returned the taps and caresses of those moving around them, who in turn touched and were touched by those on the other side of successive intermediates. Thin, wiry, small—the giants among them were under three feet—these chattering, chuttering, wrring, cooing, clicking, barking, warbling beings were constantly stroking and being stroked by each other.

From her dream, Meg smacked her lips and licked them with a dry tongue. Her eyes fluttered and opened, peering for an uncomprehending heartbeat at the woman who played with such tenderness over her face. She closed her eyes again and whimpered. The tiny woman withdrew a hand and released the clasp that held her shawl closed, revealing as she did so a bare chest and belly framed by a satiny pelt on her shoulders and back. Her lactating breasts were full and firm. She clambered onto the bed and, carefully, straddled the girl. Leaning over that chapped and bloodied mouth she pressed beside one nipple, causing a drop of milk to fall onto the girl's dry, swollen tongue. She pushed the breast onto those lips and they responded. Her milk, its thick body warm and deliciously sweet, was exhausted in moments by the hungry girl, but it was enough. A dribble at the corner of that parched mouth gleamed faintly luminous in the room's deep twilight.

Meg swallowed the first time painfully, but the second time with greater ease. The third time was weak but without apparent discomfort. Her eyes opened and she scanned the faces of those beside her bed.

She thought, "There's something odd about the bearded lady's hands."

She turned her head away and fell into dreamless sleep. This seemed to give the little people a great deal of satisfaction.

Satisfied, also, seemed the one who watched from his perch on a ladderback chair forced close to the girl by the confines of the room. He rocked the chair onto its two back legs, placing a hand on the neighboring wall for steadiness, and closed his own eyes for a count of ten.

No sooner had this watcher relaxed his vigil than one of the small folk, passing by the radio in the other room, barked sharply at the droning short-wave broadcast. It stopped and fiddled with the dials, twisting the volume sharply up and tuning in a clear signal of big band swing. As one, the little people erupted into a pulsing, boiling fusion of ancient clog and instinctual jitterbug.

Bouncing, rhythmic enthusiasm spilled a circulating current into the sick room as a continuous train of dancers flowed through the door, spreading the joy and craning to check the condition of the girl. Bedside attendants never left off their ministrations to join the revels, but as they rendered tenderly unto Meg they twitched and bopped in time to the music, all of them warbling, barking, shrilling, chattering, chuttering, wrring and whistling their own additions to the melody.

The one who had watched from the chair opened his eyes again at the crash of the song. Rising, he threaded his way through the dancing mass to the radio, beside which he patiently stood until the end of the tune. He smiled at the cavorting beings filling the space before him, even allowing himself a few snaps of the fingers and a bit of tapping of one foot. But when the piece ended, he switched the radio off and disconnected the battery. Through the sudden quiet of the music's wake he heard the passage of a late flying ouslam disappearing outside in the night.

Quickly, he crossed to the cabin's door and out into the darkness. He stopped abruptly and stood motionless, gazing up again at the long missed constellations of his native heavens.

# *Two*

𝀽

WHEN MEG SURFACED AT LAST INTO consciousness she could not identify the twitters and trills rising around her. The birdlike song she had absorbed in her sleep did not last long in any case. At the instant she became truly awake the nearest voices changed to a deep, open throated hoohooing. Like a conference of baritone owls, this new call washed out from beside her, taken up by additional voices to ripple from her bedside into the adjacent room. And yet—her brows knit ever so slightly—from out there she continued to hear the trilling song's more remote but fundamental texture.

Pats and caresses ranged over her entire body, tiny hands playing a feathery percussion. With effort, she held her eyes fully open. The light, at first so blinding, became, as her vision adjusted, the dim half-light of the cabin with no lamp burning, the shutters closed.

Moving her head was still more than she could attempt, but its angle on the pillow allowed her eyes to track the room. Beside her the bearded woman and several like her, male and female, ministered to Meg where she lay.

She focused on the bearded woman, who responded with a long, tremolant coo and a series of glancing strokes to Meg's face. Meg saw that the woman's "beard" was actually the lower, front part of a mane that framed the creature's face and grew down under her loose shawl, onto her back and shoulders.

The tiny being's face seemed not quite human. The nose was just a little too long, almost like a modest version of the pendulous nose she had once seen on a monkey in a photo from National Geographic. The eyebrows were a little too arch, the eyes deep and too liquid.

The hands surprised her so much that when she noticed them she hiccupped. From each narrow palm three long, slender fingers were opposed by two thumbs.

"Like a koala," she mouthed to herself.

Strange as the appearance of these creatures was, however, she felt safe among them. Their presence impressed her as exotic and beautiful, and their ministrations soothed her spirit, softening the bone ache and alleviating the weakness that held her down. She glanced at those clustering around the cot then looked back to the one beside her head. That one, cooing, gently turned Meg's face slightly, then reached up to separate the fastener of her shawl.

Beneath it, she wore nothing above the waist. Her mane covered her neck down to her collarbones. As much as Meg could see around the drapes of the shawl, the woman's arms, back, and sides were lightly furred. Her breasts and belly were hairless. Laying a hand to Meg's cheek, the woman leaned over and with the other squeezed one of her breasts. Two drops of milk fell on the girl's slightly parted lips. It was the sweet drink of her previous waking. When the woman leaned close and pressed her nipple to Meg's mouth, she took it in, hungry and grateful.

The tiny woman stroked Meg's hair as she suckled.

A few mouthfuls were all her nurse provided, yet the effort of feeding tired Meg quickly. Sleep waited slim moments away. The harshness in her throat shied from uttering even a whisper. With only a little more energy she thought she could muster a tentative, "Dad?" But she did feel better. Better each moment her companions stroked, patted and sang.

Under her blanket she wore what felt like a soiled diaper.

"I have to get up," she told herself, "real soon."

Later, the woman half woke her to nurse again in the dark stillness of late night. When Meg had finished, the woman climbed onto the cot and snuggled close alongside her. Meg fell back to sleep with the small figure cradled by her arm.

# *Three*

# ʔ

LONG BEAMS OF EARLY MORNING BROKE through the seams of the eastern shutters. For the first few seconds Meg's mind hung out of gear. She watched the slow drift of motes through the thin slices of light. Her nurse still nestled, sleeping against her side, a tiny creature hardly longer than her arm.

The room around her still hummed with a low, somnolent chorus of shushing respiration.

Abruptly, her mind clicked to alert as she detected a heavier, wakeful breathing in the corner behind her, away from the window. Her nurse and companions all sat up at once.

Meg, braving the pain, turned her head, mouthing, "Da..." but broke it off in the face of a stranger seated in the chair beside her bed.

His curly hair spilled into his beard from under an unbilled brocade cap. Though taller than her nurse by a good eight or nine inches, he was still remarkably short. Trim and well knit, he was also extraordinarily broad across the shoulders and chest. His hands, while wide, callused and horny, were configured with a normal arrangement of fingers and thumbs. In addition to the cap, he was clad in a shirt of red flannel and heavy trousers of some buff fabric. The pants were tucked into brown leather boots laced tightly to just below his knees. His eyes held some part of the liquid depth of her nurse.

His breath drew deep and slow.

The normally configured hands—normal, that is, in having the usual number and kinds of digits—were frozen in what looked like a stage in some peculiar version of cat's cradle. He held a string, a coarse, loose cord kept from raveling by a knot at either end. On his lap lay a pile of fiber, semi-organized into loose turns, and a stick on which was twisted more of the string, its end a delta into unspun hanks.

"Not your dad, I'm afraid." He spoke in a kind of low rumbling, his accent both thick and musical. "I go by Jack."

He winked at her.

"Jack Plenty. My cousins and I found your dad and you at death's door. You'd made it out of the cabin and you were tossing and weeping in a great fit when we came in on the vibes. Your dad was slumped onto the table next to the radio, his whole body all shaking. Ekaterina got you onto the cot there while I tried to do something for the old man."

He paused and dropped his gaze to the ground, letting his hands fall into his lap, oblivious to the tangling of the string.

"Pantisocratic fever," he observed softly. "Worst cases I've ever seen."

His eyes turned up as if referring to something on the underside of his brow, bunching the skin of his forehead.

"Some rot about genetic might-probablies and all around you, whatchacallit, Enviro's mental triggers. I don't know. It was that radio."

He jabbed an index finger emphatically toward the other room.

"Neither one of you should have been listening, not with your who-you-come-froms what they are. Especially not for years, like with this more outright stretch of the Long War."

He began trying to sort out the snarl in his lap, pulling at some loop here, another there. Progress evaded him.

"We home in on the vibrations, you know. Just sort of beam in on the fever vibes and here we are with our little tenders come to procreate and nurse."

Flicking the tangle loose, he waggled one hand to the side, as though indicating an unseen presence.

"After insemination they give up milk for two whole years before they conceive, the healing milk, like balm from Gilead..."

He kissed his fingertips.

"Like the spittle of an angel's kiss. But their bodies won't realize a fertile egg until two years done and their milk becomes the ordinary suck of pretty babes."

He winked, then shrugged.

"Okay, slightly special. Doesn't keep them from going through any motions, though. Not at all. There's no stopping them from going through any kind of motions."

His expression went from smile to frown.

"Terrible thing, though, this fever. Your case."

Leaning back, he almost looked down his nose at her.

"Mostly, this crud is the only clue we have to incipient pre-dispositional empathy traits in full humans. You know, genetic marker and all that stuff."

With his free hand he began to pick anew at the wad of string.

"Mostly." He paused, shook his head once, then went on. "Mostly, it takes shape in the wearies...and crummy gut, mild to acute. I've seen hives from time to time...and burning water. All that type of telltale."

He leaned closer.

"But a man dead and his bairn nearly so...I don't know what to make of it, I truly do not. Ekaterina probably knows. I'm a little vague on the theoreticalizing, myself. Much more the feelie type, you know?"

He was trying to tell her something, she was sure of it. He did not seem to require much from her, certainly not an articulated response. What he was saying was about her, or at least concerned her, and meant something about the state she was in. She would have to sort it out later. She tried to focus on that thought: that, later, she would have to figure out what this man was trying to say. She hoped that concentrating on a single subject would help her stay awake.

For a few seconds the ploy worked, then the dryness of her eyes became a burning and tears flooded her vision. When she blinked in reflex some trigger was tripped and she dropped toward sleep. As she fell away she heard the man saying, "I have composed a line or two on the subject, if I may be so bold."

He cleared his throat, then continued,

*"The fever pitch that burns all night..."*

Whatever came next was lost in the gulf.

# *Four*

𝓲

"...*Psychomasters! Pleasure girls bust out smiling,*
    *insincere,*
*working for wages, wanted for wages, unwilling unfulfilled,*
*strutting a highlife without satisfaction, that much is clear,*
*that much and a few other things not listed*
    *in the particular bills*
*detailing goods obtained from the leaning plazas*
    *of Bobbo's lawn,*
*Oh, babble on, fair muse, my tongue is yours as you will.*
*Atta way to call them; small or large, that is, or small..."*

She finally opened her eyes after a long struggle in which she
tried to believe the droning voice was part of a dream she could
push through to quieter sleep. It seemed this weird man had
been reciting on and on forever. Some piece of her, she realized,
had been listening to his twisting verse, but like an eavesdrop-
per more than an audience. He appeared to need nothing from
her. Even sleeping, her presence alone was enough.

"...*containerless, tinless, bootless, fruitless, of no account*
*and beloved, therefore, of the lesser gods, the odd sprite*
*splintered off from the all inclusive light of heaven's mount,*
*the Rudys of paradise, the LaVernes, their Chevies, tight*
*with all roads and steady in the spray of the many founts*
*of the demon's drool, not one whittle to pass our sight..."*

His words seemed to hammer at her—senseless, rambling,
flitting subject to subject like a nectaring insect. Unable to

follow, she tried to shut it out, to sink away from the flow of language back into unawareness. His voice persisted, never slowing even as it rose to shouts or sank to whispers in a train of emotional passes she could not connect to the words springing from his throat.

> *"...corsairs come upon the winds, great scimitars flash*
> *in the gleam of the single winking eye of voyeuristic heaven,*
> *blinking in the shifting veils of cloud, a clangor, a clash*
> *between the slight colors of natural day and the bruise*
>             *of industry's leaven*
> *mixed into our food for thought, the abutment a gash*
> *upon the reflections in our hearts of the seas, all seven*
> *ranged 'round us like a relish tray around the bowl of dip,*
> *good herbs stirred into a fatty, gelatinous liquid, sipped*
> *on the crunching chomp of those yummy sticks of celery..."*

"Shut up," she thought. "Just shut up. I want to sleep, sleep. Go away." Curling into a ball, she clapped hands tightly over her ears. He went on.

> *"...fair is as fair would have it, the briefer wings,*
> *the wing-a-dings, the catalog, so many graceful killer boys,*
> *so many ships, so many stones in the armory*
>             *of distant slings,*
> *false glories accosted amidst the attitudes of playthings, toys*
> *in the hands of giants, in these midge's hands the ringing*
> *of the bells of perdition, duck and cover. The perfume cloys,*
> *clutters, clogs the intakes, affronts the senses, perfect tension*
> *drawn out to the perfect tautness of a high string*
>             *on our lady's harp,*
> *to pluck and fondle under discretion's tarp,*
> *for as so change our attitudes so changes our grasp of this*
> *one what in a hell of creation..."*

"...Sleep. Sleep. Sleep. Sleep," she repeated as a bludgeon in her mind, a pounding mantra wall erected against the torrent of language vented by this incomprehensible Jack.

"...Sleep. Sleep. Sleep. Sleep," she timed it to the pulse in her throbbing temples.

"...Sleep. Sleep. Sleep. Sleep..."

The effort of continuing this inner chant soon exhausted her, and she slipped into enfolding dream. But the odd man's words followed her a ways, to stand just inside the boundary of waking, hailing her, then slowly fading as with distance.

# *Five*

HER EYES WERE ALREADY OPEN AND focused when her mind woke. Sharp pains came with every movement of her head, so she did not shift her gaze. Thirst, and the extreme dryness of her mouth, brought a longing for the milk she'd had before. This, in turn, caused her to realize she was alone with that peculiar man. Her nurse and the others had vanished. The room seemed oddly lit, filled with a dim, wavering, dirty golden glow.

She was looking at Jack when her thoughts restarted. He and his kit were slightly blurry, as if he were less solid...or had begun diffusing into the atmosphere. She blinked several times hoping to clear her eyes, but he would not resolve into focus. Everything else in her field of vision was sharply defined.

Jack was oblivious to her stare, lost in his own activities. He had oriented his chair so that he could prop up one leg on the wall, and there he sat, naked except for a cloth worn as a short skirt. With his right hand against his leg he was spinning more lumpy string from his twists of combed fibers. With his left hand he kept the thread tight and took it up onto his stick. Each time his hand passed along his leg he rocked forward until the chair was almost flat on the ground, and then rocked back onto the two rear legs as he took up the new slack onto the spindle. Neither his process nor his pace indicated a great concern for producing a large amount of string.

He was speaking while he spun, she realized. The merest hint of an echo followed his voice. He seemed to be composing a poem, trying different versions of phrases and sentences.

*"The gift we spin and cord and weave and sew*
*and reshape some winter afternoon as cookies*
*is the number one pipeline to what you better believe is so...*

"Wait a minute," he interrupted himself. "That line walks with a crutch. Better make that

*...is the number one pipeline to what you need to know..."*

He seemed to repeat this line silently, testing it, weighing it. Satisfied, he went on, "So, then, that makes it,

*The gift we spin and cord and weave and sew*
*and reshape some winter afternoon as cookies*
*is the number one pipeline to what you need to know,*
*The Big One, the pro who shows that you and me are rookies,*
*a kindness against a beat-you-down life's unnervings,*
*a balm because the hearts of seekers readily bruise.*

"Now that's what I call a working first verse," he congratulated himself. "Which brings us to the second verse. Let me see. Good poetry always moves from thought to action. The first one was pretty thoughtful, if I say so myself. Took me a deal of thinking, anyway. So, then, what kind of action? But there's only one action right for The Big One, right? So that's easy."

With a flourish, he declaimed,

*"Consequently, let me put this sacred gift, this grass,*
*fair communion, into the bowl of my Chaldean chalice*
*blown of a creamy, opalescent glass*
*and fit for suction by all who forego malice*
*toward the world of each-and-every's birthing,*
*which is to say, lovers of the greeny muse."*

At this, he pulled from his bag a chambered instrument to which a long hose was attached. The top of it looked like a small eggcup with what appeared to be soot around its edge. Jack removed this, revealing that the cup was the head of a narrow pipe that ran to the lower of the two chambers of the device. The device itself was, as Jack's poem had said, of a creamy, opalescent glass, although dark with what seemed an internal discoloration. He separated the two chambers, opening the lower. From his bag he took a small flask, from which he first filled the chamber with a transparent, amber liquid, then poured a healthy swallow down his own throat. This caused him to cough and his eyes to tear.

"Oh, stuff me!" he said, "but that is good!"

He stowed the flask and closed the now liquid filled lower chamber, which he refitted to its mate. This upper piece he opened, removing from inside a small wad of moist, leafy matter. After closing the upper chamber, and adjusting the hose that emerged from its top, he pressed the leafy matter into the little cup on the end of its pipe and reinserted the pipe into the larger instrument.

For a moment he raised the device as if in offering to someone unseen, closed his eyes and mumbled something beneath his breath. Then he stuck the end of the hose in his mouth, produced a lit match by sleight of hand, and then held the flame to the little cup while noisily puffing. In a moment the cup glowed with the presence of a steady coal. Jack inhaled slowly while shaking out the match. He held his breath until his face turned red. When he exhaled the room filled with a thick, pungent smoke. He took another long pull on the hose, held it again, blew another heavy cloud into the room. At this point he noticed Meg watching him.

"Hello," he said, his hand rising and falling in an exaggerated slow motion wave. "You're awake. Have a taste of the ol' communion chalice?"

Meg's throat no longer seemed familiar with the process of making words. She tried to speak, but could only struggle out, "What...what?"

"What is it?" Jack finished for her. "Well you should ask," he went on, "because this is no ordinary offered thing. Not for old Jack Plenty. Brought this from seed to sacrifice my own self, grown for flower not for fiber. Strictly religious. My own small measure of diplomatic reception of the ineffable intelligence of the immanent all. Uh, 'God' you might call it, the all that is, not the offered thing. That's more in the nature of a supply of prayers, you know. Not the prayers like spinning and weaving, but the other kind, the floaters. Sure you won't have a go?"

Meg moved her head in the least possible arc of a negative shake, at which Jack produced another match and helped himself to a third puff. The smoke hung thickly in the small room. It seemed to be making her dizzy. Only it wasn't dizzy, but something else, some other sensation she had no name for. She wasn't even sure if it was unpleasant. But whatever the effect was, it combined with the weakness that already held her to bed and made it that much harder to draw herself together. Completely limp upon the low cot, she slipped away from awareness of the room into an imagining that was some part waking fantasy but through which she watched herself move as though in dream. She was walking, sometimes skipping, down a wooded lane, humming the melody to a dance tune she'd heard on the radio. The light came through the trees blue and gold. She was content to continue along the lane as she followed it down toward authentic sleep. Just before she stepped across the border into oblivion she thought that the leafy stuff in Jack's water pipe must be marijuana.

"But that would be illegal," was her last waking thought.

# Six

"LIKE I WAS SAYING, THOUGH, you two are a puzzle." Jack accented this statement with a grave nod of the head. "Is it this piece of war? We see it as just another phase in the struggle, no meaner or worse than what you call peace. No fewer victims that's for sure, but to you it's a more acute state. And from your point of view it's been a long separation from what you tell yourself is peace."

To underscore the authority of his words, he squinted one eye and leaned forward.

"Oh, I know, 'A subjective influence is consistent with incipient predispositional empathy.' I know the drills. But is it that or is it something about your particular mix of come-befores and the specific empathic predispositions incipient in you? Didn't think I could get that one out of my mouth, did you?"

A radiant gloat bounced into his expression.

"It's not the words that give me fits. The words heel fine enough. It's the notions themselves that get hazy and soft. See what I'm saying?"

His tone was redolent with sincerity.

"I mean, is this merely the first two cases of a soon to be global outbreak of some especially nasty strain of pantisocratic fever—brought on by subjective response to a perceived fact of total industrial war, maybe—or is it just something peculiar and unseen about you?"

Rolling back his head, he looked down his nose at her.

"Observe the masterly choice of words. Like I was saying, could you be, maybe, the most iconoclastic possibility for matrilineal-type infiltration since, for instance, the Blessed Virgin

Mary? Or, after all, only one of a scad of wordshapes in a pleasant tale?"

As he had talked, Jack had been working the pile of fiber that sat again in his lap. His left hand held the spindle, onto which he would take up the lumpy, irregular string produced as he rolled the fiber against his leg. He was fully clad: boots, trousers, shirt, cap.

The tiny woman slept cuddled beside Meg, although—as if responding to being noticed—she now sat up and looked from side to side, blinking owlishly.

Again Meg tried to speak.

"You...that smoke...," she began.

"Smoke?" Jack asked, giving her a puzzled look.

"That smoke," she repeated, "that...that stuff you were smoking...what?"

"I'm afraid you got me, sister," he answered. "I don't really know what you're talking about."

"Before. I woke up. Your poem. You were smoking. Was it...was it marijuana?"

Jack pulled back, a shocked look on his face. In a moment he regained his composure. His eyebrows rose high as he spoke in forceful tones.

"I'm not going to pretend I'm unfamiliar with the term," he assured her, "or even unacquainted with the practice you mention," he slapped a fist into the other, open palm, "but I'm telling you, when you're serious about making a change in the prevailing order there are certain, ah, practices that you put aside in the interest of the, whatchacallit, revolutionary moment."

"Plus, it's illegal," Meg croaked.

"Hah!" Jack barked a guffaw. "Illegal! Sister, of course it's illegal. It has a thousand practical uses, grows in desert or ditch, and can take the edge from a seeker's pain."

Scrunching closed an eye, he jabbed an index finger for emphasis.

"Every prohibition is about two things. One is to say who yanks tight the reins on harvesting wealth from ordinaries like you and yours truly. The other is making plain folks into criminals and largening up the powers of the police. Which is very convenient when you're a bigwig not sure whose head you'll want to crack, see what I'm saying? No," he smirked as at a choice joke, "Prohibitions should be resisted, not obeyed. No," he waved a finger in the air, taking a more serious tone, "the reason to set aside such observances is because the times require us to look sharp and think fast, and act when the moment is ripe. See?"

Meg stared at him coolly.

"So, not marijuana?" she pressed despite her raspy throat.

"Not to any knowledge of mine," he stated unequivocally.

"What...then, what?"

"I have to say again, I don't know what you're talking about."

Jack looked straight into her eyes as he said this, holding her gaze for several seconds. She broke off, and looked away. Her throat ached from producing so many words.

He fell into a reverie, his eyes on a point somewhere beyond the wall, his broad hand stroking his chin. He sat like this for a long minute, then returned to himself with a start.

"Pantisocratic fever, we call it. Terrible thing of ague and chills, delirium, pertussis, phlegm and catarrh, rheum from the eyes and thrashing, all that in you and only you. In your old dad the rigidity and seizures, followed by an abrupt cessation of symptoms of any kind. In a word, death. That's what you call it. We call it something else entirely. Something like a broken heart." As if in illustration, his chest heaved with a tremendous sigh. However, he warmed again as he continued explaining. "It's when grief and anger at the senselessness and destruction spill over and become physically, you know, manifest? Real anyway. We can feel it, and we come with the little ones, their— hah hah!—procreative urges, and their milk. We are here."

At this last statement he paused, leaning forward as though awaiting her words. She drew together her strength and croaked, "Why—?"

"Why? You ask why? Why, to pull the world back from the brink. To seek an end to the folly and a beginning to regeneration."

He leaned back, satisfied, as though releasing her. She fought to keep herself conscious, hanging on to a fleeting observation that he spoke like a government clerk trying to sound important. Suddenly, a cloud seemed to pass over the man's face, and he lurched forward again.

"I fear I gave him no more than quiet of mind and ease of body as he departed. I'm sorry."

It took her a moment to understand this referred to her father. Her father was dead. This strange man had been saying that.

Soon after sitting up, her tiny nurse had climbed off the cot and resumed patting and stroking Meg. She had been joined almost immediately by others spilling in through the door and taking up positions around the cot, all patting and stroking while the larger girl attended to the things Jack said. They hoohooed at Meg and each other, mixing in some of the parakeet-like twitters and trills that seemed to fill the adjoining room. The realization that her father was dead coincided so exactly with an abrupt change in the song of the small people that she was startled. She heard an air of consolation enter their voices. She felt it in her body, felt the song of these strange little creatures bathing the chasmic loss that had so suddenly hit home.

"Me?" she strained to ask. "I made them change?"

"Well, ah. Yeah."

For a moment he did not seem inclined to say any more, but then continued, "Well, someone will have to explain it all sometime, and it won't be easier for the putting off."

Jack shrugged his shoulders up beneath his ears, dropping them again with an explosive exhalation.

"First, You cannot know how much I wish I'd had more to do for your Dad."

She blinked as tears gathered at the corners of her eyes.

"What?" she asked. "Where?"

"Kate, ah, Kate, that is, Ekaterina and I buried him at the head of the meadow."

"Ekaterina." She motioned toward her small nurse with her eyes. "Her?"

Jack giggled.

"No," he said. "No, but old Kate wouldn't be upset that you might've thought so." He interrupted himself with a snicker. "No, Kate, I call her 'Kate,' but only when she's not within listening. Ol' Kate's been gone for two, two-and-a-half days, arranging for food. I expect her back today or tomorrow. Or the next day. It's hell for provisions with all this warring. As for the little one there next to you, how she knows herself or her kind is their mystery, but we call her 'Sweetheart.' Even among folks like hers who live to be kind she stands out for her kindness. Kind to me more than once. More ways than one. You better believe it."

Meg turned to look at the being beside her. "Sweetheart" hoohooed and twittered and trilled, and stroked the girl's face, and tapped lightly on her arm and upper chest. Occasionally, the tiny woman turned to tap or stroke or sing to the creature beside her, itself similarly engaged. The tightness and pain in Meg's throat began to fade.

She turned back to Jack and asked, "Who are they? I mean, are they people?"

He screwed up his face in a rapid sequence of expressions suggesting confusion, irritation, discomfort and—ultimately—determination.

"Who they are...I mean, who they are," he finally said, "is, well, your kinfolk. Or ours. Some of us closer than others. I mean, like you to me so me to them. See?"

Jack paused and seemed to re-taste the words that he had chosen. Meg could see satisfaction move over his face as he decided that this beginning addressed whatever reservations he had about discussing the beings around them. He went on.

"Them, you, me, we're all one big dog-cluster evolution-wise. Or not evolution-wise, that's not right. It's that DNA stuff. Genes, that's it. Gene-wise we're just like dogs and foxes and coyotes. Whatsit? Ol' Kate's got a phrase, like this,"

Jack sat bolt upright and intoned, "'Closely related but differentiable species able to hybridize fertilely.'"

He relaxed and continued, "Us Intuits are a mite freer with our tongues and we say 'dog-cluster.'"

He paused for a moment as his hands became entangled in the string he was spinning. He extricated them with a flick, then began picking at the resulting tangle.

"Or some such. You know, like dogs and wolves. You cross them you get wolf-dogs for the generations. Cross a horse and a donkey, now, you get a mule. A human and some others, you get a mule. A tiger and a lion, you get a mule. What Kate says is 'offspring with no possibility of successive issue.' What a bunch of words for mule. You know what that 'issue' means? Gets me all bothered just considering it."

Meg noticed Jack's left hand kneading his crotch as he talked. Never before had she encountered an adult male who would do such a thing in the middle of a conversation. It frightened her. It also made her angry. At the same time, she realized he did

not really seem to be aware he was giving himself an obvious
erection. Jack's hand seemed possessed of independent life as
he continued his explanation.

"But, you know, our friends here, all of them, and me and
mine, too. And you and yours. Us, we're all a dog-cluster.
Mix us up and we have happy little babies all set to grow up
and mix it some more. That's the long and short of the big-
gest plan, you know. To mix as much of them and as much
of mine into you and yours as can be done. That way, we'll
stop all this warring, or slow it down, and change you for all
of forever. When you're more recovered we'll be all set to do
some serious mixing, don't you know?"

He punctuated this with several leering winks. Meg was
taken aback. She had worked hard to ignore the enlarging
evidence of Jack's sexual energy as it grew under his left
hand's ceaseless action, but this last statement of his made
that evidence a looming threat.

"Are you going to rape me?" she asked, struggling to
keep her voice from breaking.

"Me? No! No, you got it wrong! I never would!" He
waved away the thought with his unoccupied hand. "No, I'm
here for these friends of mine, these, uh, whatchacall'ems,
you got a word for them, you know, technically 'homuncular
empaths' they suggest back at training, but your folks have
a word, you know from old times, whatsit? Um, once com-
monly but not so common since we had to take them out
of this neck of Being for their protection. You haven't had
much opportunity to see them. But your ancestors did." He
snapped his fingers several times as he searched his memory.
His eyes lit up. "Right! 'Elves.' Their word for these folk was
'elves.'"

Meg stopped herself before she began, "There's no such
thing as—"

Before now she had had no inkling there existed any such
beings as these. They were indisputably real and present. Or
she was indisputably lost in a broad hallucination. Whichever
way that argument went, 'elfish' was not a bad description
for the small figures clustered around her bed. And she could
not maintain the mental category of 'creatures.' They were
just too much in their small, birdy-singing way people.

A part of her noted Jack had shifted the subject rather than directly address her fear of being assaulted. She resented this, although she felt she had little choice but to take his denial at face value. Even so, she was curious about the elves.

"Do you know their language?" she asked. "Can you talk to them?"

"Language? Oh, they don't have one of those, not like you're thinking," Jack said. "They're, whatchacallit, empaths. Quote, 'able to directly experience the emotional states of sentient entities in near proximity.' That Kate, she lets the tail wag the dog with those words of hers sometimes. Claims there's a direct relating between the size of your vocabulary and the breadth of your character. I don't think so. I hope not, at least." He gave her a conspiratorial wink. "Anyway, their minds are all grouped up, you know. I mean, they're born feeling what everyone around them feels, which just kind of leaves grammar out of the big circle of necessaries. I don't think they're really even individuals the same as you or me. I mean, you can tell them apart and they have, like, um, personalities and different ones with different talents. And preferences, even. But it's like all different faces of one picture or something, each one a part or piece of what they all are together."

Meg was straining. She was still weak and achy, and Jack's explanations were tiring her rapidly.

"I'm not really sure I understand."

"Lands, I don't wonder. It's more than I can keep in mind. The sort of thing you need to get from ol' Kate for details. There is some understanding them, though. I mean, after a while you get so you recognize some of the churring and wrrring are words, but not every kind of word. All of their words are, um, nouns or, ah...ah, words that tell you what your nouns are like..."

"Adjectives?" Meg offered.

"The very same," Jack replied, letting go of his crotch in order to make a two handed gesture, as though presenting her utterance back to her.

"But a lot of it's not words, either," he continued. "A lot of that sound goes to work right on your brain. Like your ears carry it to places where words don't mean anything but where those sounds just fit right in and cause your head to send out the right signals to get the rest of you to fix yourself. You're probably not aware of it, but the whole time they're singing they're also giving off special smells. Not knock you in the face smells, but delicate, like an old sachet still in the wardrobe from last season. Quote, 'directly psychoactive vocalizations and complex pheromonal releases.' More of that stuff from Ekaterina's big, fat book. The way they touch you is important, too. A Chinese doctor of my acquaintance said that they just seem born knowing all about life energy flowing, you know, chi, or whatchacallit, qi or whatever. They can tell when it's blocked somewhere inside of you and they know just how to touch you to get it moving again. A big piece of why you're feeling better now instead of dead.

"Not that there's anything wrong with dead," he added. "Just that quick is better."

One of the elves, another female, came up beside Jack's chair and begun to twitter softly, touching him about the face, chest and arms. Jack responded by gently stroking her head with his right hand, but other than that showed no change of attention. His left hand had long since returned to his crotch. His voice barely paused.

"Hear this, their spit kills germs, and at special times, like Sweetheart now, the women give milk that can cure most kinds of sickness. All the tools they've ever had are the sticks most of them carry, and they'd walk naked in their nice fur coats if we didn't give them skirts and shawls against the fire and ice of the elements. What finally tipped the balance, though, is the fact that they just have to try to love and hug us out of our funks. They don't have funks, you can imagine, and we're all right—mine are that is; the ones I live with—but oh, you humans, you break a brother's heart. When we parsed it out and got a full view of the slave life and torment that humans would give them, well, that did it. We had to do something. We were going ourselves, so we took them along when we vacated the consensus. It was all we could do. 'Course, they, like us, have to come back to this sorry state of affairs to actually conceive in our procreative..." he nudged in her direction with an elbow and leered, "...cycles. I say, 'we,' but you should know, I'm three-eighths human, mother's side—she whose granddad was a randy elf. Or 'thrm.' That's my word for them, thrm'm, not elves. Of course, father's side, that half of me is all dvarsh and worthy of the mention."

As Meg had listened she had drowsed back toward sleep, her small reserves spent by her brief part in the exchange and the still unprocessed loss of her father. For as long as she could she held herself at the farthest outpost of alertness to which Jack's voice could reach. When even that effort became too great, she slept.

# Seven

THE WAY SHE WOULD REMEMBER IT later is that he was before her when she opened her eyes.

Meg came awake, if she did wake, less fully and with more distress than before. She felt pressed down by a force that she perceived apart from her physical weakness. A force like intensifying gravity, but also something like a wind, it was a steady blow that brought great heaviness to her. Movement was so difficult she felt frozen in place.

She could not raise her head to look around the darkened room. From the corners of her eyes she could see the elf creatures all deeply and utterly sleeping. The only light in the room came from directly in front of her. Jack was there, perched naked upon the chair in an erect squat, his arms up, hands claw-like, the fingers wiggling. His eyes shone with a boiling mix of orange and gold. Around his body a dim halo of the same colors fluxed, seeming to coalesce into Jack or in some other way share his substance. Later she would remember shapes, buildings, a landscape in that nimbus, remember it as the bilious orange clouds and yellow sky of a great city that sprawled transparently over the room to every horizon.

In the moment, she was more aware of Jack. He stared at her fixedly, a leering grin pasted to his face. His penis was hugely erect and pointed directly at her. The gravity wind seemed to emanate from Jack's cock and wiggling fingers.

She became acutely aware of her degree of nakedness under the sheet and blanket. She felt the covers begin to inch down her body, or even slower than that, creep a millimeter, a mil, a smidgen at a time. Her nipples began to harden under the slow thread-by-thread friction of the cotton sheet.

She could not move. She could make no sound other than a rattling sigh. Jack's tongue shot from between his teeth and flicked like a serpent's. His eyebrows bobbed wildly up and down. She felt like she was being licked on every spot the hands of an elf had touched. The constancy of the force began to nauseate her. She fled again into the waiting black.

# *Eight*

"NOW, YOU TAKE ME FOR INSTANCE, Jack Plenty."

Meg had no idea how long Jack had been talking. She struggled out of sleep as out of a faint, and with the sense that it had been the persistent droning of Jack's voice that had drawn her to wakefulness.

"Or, Jackanapes Plenty, if you want the giving-witness form. Now me, as I was saying before, I'm three-eighths human, and proud of it, you better believe. But all the same, half dvarsh. And not just any dvarsh, mind you, but a Rigidstick of the Nondifferential clan. Very prestigious, cadet or not."

He gave her a look that challenged her to disbelieve him. She suddenly realized her diaper was clean and the sheets on her cot were fresh. Memory of her experience of naked Jack and the gravity wind, or her vision of same, or dream or whatever, returned.

"What did you do to me last night?" she demanded.

"Ah, do?" Jack responded.

"When you were on that chair. With that beam or ray. That wind. Whatever it was. What were you doing to me?"

"Ah, sister. I do not know of what you speak. My main activity in the night was sawing logs, don't you know? Lost in the cinema on my eyelids."

"Did you change my clothes?" she asked, refusing to let go of her suspicion.

"Me, no. Kate popped in and did that. You were out like an empty lantern. I was told if I wasn't going to help I should stay in the other room. Kate says you have a lot of body taboos. Now like I was saying—"

"Who is Kate?" Meg interrupted him. "Why does she only come here when I'm unable to see her?"

"Why, Kate is Ekaterina," Jack answered. "Grandchild of my grandam. You know, my cousin. She has quite a few arrangements to make, and so she had to go off and make them. But she comes by to keep an eye on things. She'll be here to stay before you know it."

He gave her a great leering wink, followed by an arch look, then a slack-jawed grin. Meg watched him without a word. It was at least a day's trek from anything like civilization. The location was not exactly one that allowed for abrupt popping in or out. The thought of a story, that Jekyll and Hyde story (or was it Heckle and Jeckle?), slipped into her mind but she quickly suppressed it. She didn't know if her nocturnal experience had been what she was used to thinking of as real or not. She could set that aside. The Kate or Ekaterina story was more troubling, for she had only Jack as a source for it, and only that story to account uncomfortably for her cleaner state. While she could not readily accept the account as true, she needed, for the moment at least, not to decide outright it was untrue.

"Like I was saying," Jack went on, "I may do some real human stuff, like improvise, or skylark, and I may be slack at the mathemagics, you know, and, ah, say...vague, too, on some of the 'pataphysics, but hey, I can jump with the best of them. No eigenstate can hold me. And the way I think, most of the stuff I like, the way I see things, that's all dvarsh, which is how we call ourselves. Your kind say 'dwarf.' Not that I'm not proud of my human parts. Like I said before, I'm just pleased as pudding about it, and about Old Pop, too, my great-granddaddy from the Thrm. Great-grandmama's the one who named him Old Pop. They died together, him in her arms, and I've accounted her a happy woman. That's why I say take me for example. I'm some of each and all together, Dvarsh and Human and Thrm. The very best example, if I say so myself, of harmonious coexistence. That's why I'm in on it. That's why I save the sum of my goodly acts to raising the human heel from the throat of our ancestral home consensus. I made a poem about it."

He drew himself up, squared his shoulders.

"Please, no," Meg said. "I'm afraid I'm still too tired to follow one of your poems."

"No?" confirmed Jack, more redirected than interrupted. "I use lots of the old words, the old human words: human, dwarf, elf. I like using those words. They make me think of a time when humans had room for something in the world besides human things. Kate and Mattie, that's Mathilde, Kate's sister, and Kate is, of course, Ekaterina, those two had a long palaver and out of it decided these old words would work best to give you something to wrap an idea around. Contrary to what the ol' stuffies suggested back in training."

"Mathilde. Now who is Mathilde? Ekaterina's sister and what else?"

"Did I forget to say her before? She's important. The third of our Three Out Of Four."

"Three outer whats?"

"A Three Out Of Four. I jerk my thumb over my shoulder and say 'Tee-double-o-eff' just for the fun of its fit to the tongue but that kind of abbreviating does surely piss Kate off. To her it's laziness. But that Three Out Of Four, that's what we call a basic cell. You know, what's that word? Ah, cadre?" He nodded. "Yep. Our smallest organizational unit of cadre. After one, of course. Three's the number. Mathilde's the third of us, if you count me first since I'm here..."

He gave her a broadly theatrical wink.

"...and Ekaterina as second since she's come and gone but due again."

He now lowered his voice and leaned forward conspiratorially.

"Ol' Mat's on special assignment. Probably for the duration."

She felt some of the strength go out of her.

"Every time I ask you a question, you say more things I don't understand. You're making my head hurt."

Appearing as if on cue, Sweetheart walked into the room and directly to the head of Meg's cot. She positioned herself so that her fingers could play over the young woman's shoulders, face and crown. Meg, for her part, willingly gave herself to the pleasure of these soothing explorations.

"I tell you what," Jack said. "Since you're busy with the darling there I think I'll stroll outside and see how luck has it going with old Jack Plenty."

"Who's the fourth?" Meg spoke from behind closed eyes.

"What's that?" the little man's nut-brown ears perked up.

"If you're three out of four, who's the fourth?"

A smirk unseen by his questioner spread over Jack's face.

"The fourth could be bad," he answered.

"Bad? Why?" Meg's inflection was leveling out as her relaxation went deeper.

"It's the chance you take. That's why three's the number."

"Why?" Meg was too relaxed to put the edge of irritation to her voice a piece of her felt his evasiveness warranted.

"Because three out of four isn't."

"Isn't what?"

"Bad. Isn't bad."

"Are you kidding?" Her intonation made the question sound disinterested, academic.

"Dead serious."

"So, who is the fourth?" She was unsure whether or not she actually spoke these last words.

"Later," Jack said. "Now is time to float with the touch of the hands of the little dear one."

Meg moaned once softly as a dense constriction in her scalp released under Sweetheart's persistent pushes, pats and infinitesimal petting. Jack moved out of the room, sending one long arm back behind him to snag the door and pull it shut.

Sweetheart chuttered and wrred and massaged Meg's head until the young woman was breathing regularly and slowly. Then the thrm began to rain the lightest, most feathery taps of her fingertips around, about and on Meg's face, to a sensation and effect that the human found oddly familiar.

"...like the kiss not meant to wake the child, in thousands..." her thought faded before concluding.

She lost track of time, had no sense at all of time either passing or standing still.

The ease she felt went so deeply into all parts of her body that it would have taken a titanic effort to open her eyelids, part her lips to speak, twitch a muscle. Even to heed the input of her senses was more than she was willing to do. But her mind was awake, even alert.

She could almost see the words of her stream of silent comment forming in the blackness, and when she strained to better see them she began to see patterns, or a single, larger pattern, forming in space. A living pattern, moving, evolving, like an oriental rug of tremendous complexity, ever changing, it gave a character to the space around whichever part of her it was that watched her mind working, became the medium through which flew the silent vibrations of the words of ceaseless comment that some part of her selfhood kept lobbing past the rest.

As she watched, the pattern seemed to grow more substantial, its colors brighter, its changes more intricate, ever more fascinating. At the same time the silent voice grew distant and tinny, and still fainter, until it was a microscopic buzzing, intermittent, gone to a place far from the part of her that watched the pattern dance. From its far reach came whirling back a raw chunk of wording that she could not have read or spoken until later, when she remembered it as something seen, a series of letters twirling into the heart of the pattern, there to send out exploratory tendrils that laced into the churning evolution of living motif as itself, the phrasm, dissolved into the raw materials birthing the flow. She remembered it as lingering in an afterimage upon the liquid inflorescence of her mind:

*icandy*

# Nine

ﭐ

"SO LET ME GET THIS STRAIGHT."

Meg was now sitting up in bed, propped on her pillow and a rolled-up blanket, showing a great determination to understand what Jack was telling her.

"What you're saying is that these little people things like Sweetheart, these thrms—"

"Ah, no," Jack interrupted, "One thrm. The Thrm. Two thrm'm. No thrms, though. Ever."

"Thrm'm, then," the word seemed to tickle her mouth as she spoke it, and she smiled, "these thrm'm are—what did you say we'd call them, homonoids?"

"Humaloids, homonids, hominy. Something such."

"Homo-somethings, then. And they're so close to..." she paused before articulating the word deliberately, "humans that, even though they look so different, they can interbreed with us?"

"Correctamundo," Jack replied.

When he had come back in, red faced, swaggering, giving off a faint sweat-like odor that she thought must be the after-smell of sex, Meg realized she had been lying, eyes open, staring at the ceiling, thinking nothing. There was no sign of Sweetheart. Meg had no idea at what point her caregiver had left, nor how long had elapsed since Jack had gone out earlier. The image of this weird man having sex with one of these elf-people disturbed her. She was unable to bring herself to visualize it, and thought, consequently, that it must be a terrible thing.

"Unless," she'd suddenly thought, "it wasn't with one of them at all."

She had been relaxed, she realized, into total incapacity. Suppose he had gone out only until Sweetheart's therapies had taken her to that point where words retreat. Suppose he had been in the room before to make use of her in her helplessness and left again, returning for a second time now as her awareness refocused.

She wondered what combination of hurts would tell.

The sense of her aches, however, was that they spoke of diminished but persistent fever, and she felt too purely refreshed by her recent release to be convinced that her helplessness had been violated. Jack's manner, when she attended to it, seemed in a way she could not articulate to suggest that his inclinations lingered with another. She decided to put this fear away and see what she could learn from pressing the conversation.

Jack had seated himself immediately, and drawn out his fiber and his spindle. As he and Meg talked his hands moved, constantly spinning and taking up the coarse, uneven thread he used in his string games. He often stabbed the air with the spindle to emphasize a point, and he would occasionally draw the thread out in a wide shrug that seemed to say she was raising questions he had never asked himself. The thread, she noticed, was loose and variable to such an extreme it was surprising it even held together. He was, she decided, not a very good spinner.

Nor had he been either accomplished or direct in giving an account of the little people around them. She was still not entirely sure she had understood exactly the attempted explanation that he had overlaid, twisted up and digressed away from often.

"So, they don't really have individual minds? And they don't have a real language? You're saying their thinking and communicating are basically the same thing?" She continued her review of the pieces she'd been able to glean from his efforts at elucidation.

"Um, well. That would count close enough for points in competition. Tossing games and the like."

Meg's mouth opened, then closed. She looked doubtfully back at him.

"Tossing games?"

"Sure." Jack hunched forward in his chair, his hands pantomiming actions of a nature she could not begin to guess. "Like Cats and Old Shoes. Or Fatman's pie."

Her color rose, but she managed to keep her voice level when she asked, "What do shoes and pies have to do with what we're talking about?"

"Well, because close counts in games like that," he answered. "And what you were saying is close enough to accurate that it would have counted for something if we'd been playing one of them instead of talking. See what I'm saying?"

Meg regarded him steadily for a moment before she said anything more.

"So, the way they communicate is by feeling each other's emotional states and by singing and whistling and by the different ways that they touch special places on each other's bodies? Is that right?"

She raised her chin as she spoke in order to watch Jack's hands. His fingers had seemed to attack of their own volition the snarl resulting from his gesticulations of a moment before

"I think it's the kinds of pressure that's important, really," he told her. "And the kind of, ah, reaction that a pressure might get, you know, rather than any, um, symbolical meaning to the kinds of touching. I mean, without a language or private ownself you're not likely to share a whole lot of what they call metaphiers, see. But pretty much, yeah, that's how they do it. That and some other sort of borderline almost extra senses of which I have received, like the knowledge of, whatchacallit, proximate emotions, but an inkling."

Jabbing his spindle at her in emphasis he snagged his fingers in a loop that required a moment's attention to carefully extricate.

"And people like me, we call them 'elves', right?" Meg prompted, somewhat impatiently.

"Well, actually, that's just a word for them in your language, and not the only one. And not really accurate in terms of what you and yours think it's supposed to mean, but all the same it's them that your old ones meant when they began the saying of it. The misunderstandings arose later in explaining to those who never directly knew the kindness of the dears."

Meg was pleased that she was able, at least, to follow what everything in their conversation referred to, even as she remained not entirely clear about the bigger picture. Biology was one of her special passions, and she had been a top student in both English and Debate at the foothills high school she had just graduated. Her mind was alert and active in the same way she experienced during the most extemporaneous and daring parts of a debate contest. Her body was still weak from her illness, but recovering at a rate that she found somewhat unnerving in its rapidity.

She didn't know what she thought of her situation. She didn't want to think at all about her father being dead. She didn't even know how to think about the implications of a world that suddenly contained a goodly sized tribe of little creatures out of musty legends. What she could do was sort very carefully through this peculiar man's version of the facts. It seemed to her all-important to understand what this man was saying had happened to her, and how he and his companions had come to her aid.

"Now, you said you don't usually live here among," she paused in unconscious emphasis, "humans."

She was, of course, familiar with this term. It designated her species, her kind, she knew, but it was still an unfamiliar way to talk about it in a conversation outside a classroom. "People" was probably the label she would have been most comfortable using, but Jack made it clear that to him that term meant more than just the single kind self-designated Homo sapiens. Besides humans and these elves, and this other group he called dvarsh, she had gotten the impression that his idea of people even included apes of Africa and Asia, and a "shy giant" as he called it that migrated between Asia and North America. That could only be the "abominable snowman." Or what her dad had called "Sasquatch" or "Bigfoot."

She could feel this level of alertness fatiguing her, but she was determined to understand at least the words this person said, even if she was not yet prepared to accept entirely the reality of her circumstances. Her concentration seemed to perturb the ministering beings clustered to her cot, provoking from them a great stir of tapping and stroking of her body and an equal measure of whistling, whirrs and clicks. Sweetheart stood by her head, using her hand as a comb to Meg's hair.

"No," Jack was saying. "No, we don't usually live among you, not since the Great Disasseveration. Except we must, all of us who left, dvarsh and thrm'm and remnants of some others, even humans, a couple, return to this consensus to conceive. And to stage the goodly acts toward a grand and happy some-day return. The Struggle, you know?"

"What do you mean, return to this consensus? You talk like you don't really inhabit this world, but you don't talk about it like you come back from another planet."

"No. No, ha!" Jack suddenly got very fidgety. "It's not really about planets, no. Before too long you'll come up on the limit of planets and I look forward to that day with a mix of fear and hope. Maybe it'll shock you out of that terrible need to have. What Ol' Kate calls the 'acquisitive fallacy.' Maybe not. Could be you'll just turn your grabby hands across the planes. Ha! Could be you'll become even nastier as a threat against us, I don't know. I've jumped 'states where it's played out that way." He paused to shudder. "Not a pretty sight."

Meg looked almost angry as her brow furrowed at the strain of trying to remain abreast of his stream of talk.

"Which states did something?" she asked too sharply.

"Not states like stupid countries. Or pieces of stupid coun-tries. Reality shapes. Slices of the vast unending. Particularities among the choices of infinite multiples."

He suddenly made a motion as if plucking something from the air and then vigorously shook his closed hand, from which came a high clatter. Without preliminary, he dropped to the floor and threw what looked like three dice so they bounced lightly off the wall at a point Meg could not readily see.

"Dark of the Moon and Void of Space," Jack intoned as he swept the objects from the floor and into his pocket, "Stand Still, Do Nothing. I don't think I'm doing this right. I don't think I want to talk about this anymore."

"Is something wrong?"

For a heartbeat, she thought he was going to ignore her question.

"I think you're tired. You've been sick, you know." He suddenly flushed, his cheeks taking on a boiled look. "It's the consequences, see. I always forget about those unforeseen con-sequences. You'd better go to sleep now."

"I don't want to go to sleep yet," Meg objected. "I feel like I almost got what you were saying. What consequences are you talking about? Why stand still? Why do nothing?"

"One wrong word and I might screw the future. It all came back to me a minute ago. I say something; you hear something else. You make some choices, the drift of the consensual fabric curves to nestle those choices, right? And it's too much. The fabric rips, you know, and chaos reigns. Death rages and all is lost. See what I'm saying? See what I mean?"

He seemed to her abruptly sad and weary, his whole frame sagging in defeat. He peered into her eyes with a tenderness she found disquieting.

"Go to sleep," he told her.

"Are you saying you won't talk to me anymore?" she persisted.

He barked a guffaw.

"Not before I've had a chat with that ante-gnome, Determinism."

With that Jack got up from his chair, shoved his spinning things back into his bag, and walked out of the room. The thrm'm, elves, tender darlings, clustered around her more closely, and more came into the room to join those ministering at her bed. They pulled her covers away and removed her diaper. En masse and over her entire body they began the rain of feathery taps that Sweetheart had used earlier on her face. Meg startled herself with a hiccupping sob that burst out of her like a concentrated knot of grief. Almost instantly, she went limp and fell into sleep.

# *Ten*

)o

MEG LAY FOR SOME TIME IN a drowse, not quite waking, never quite falling asleep. A part of her was aware that it was early morning, early in the first hour of still somewhat provisional light. She was never alert enough to take in that the room, indeed, the cabin, was empty. Exhaustion maintained her in this neutral state, out of reach of nightmare and not attending to the world. She lay motionless, inert, her body too heavy and weak even to twitch or shift.

Suddenly, she came fully awake. Her hair began to prickle and rise on her head, her neck, the backs of her arms that were under her covers.

She tried to call out, "hello!" but managed little better than a croak as her throat tightened with alarm. The sense of charge, its intensity, grew.

From the next room came a loud, abrupt clap, a number of successive blue flashes and a smell of ozone. A wisp of gray smoke floated through the doorway. There was a moment of silent stillness, then the sounds of someone moving around beyond her open door, apparently examining the cabin's furnishings and content. The person seemed to proceed with a great deal of thoroughness.

Meg lay as though frozen, but her mind raced. This was obviously not Jack and not an elf-being. Fear began to fill her. She was incapable of flight, had no strength for struggle, very likely could not even raise herself from the cot on which she lay beginning to hyperventilate.

A man, apparently human, walked into the room, stopped in the middle, and turned completely around surveying it. He wore a military uniform of a kind that Meg had never before seen. The tunic was a bright, light green, the color of lime sherbet. Down its front ran a great deal of gold filigree in an irregular, angular network of branching lines and terminating circles. The pants were of a clinging, stretchy material that showed off his muscular legs. His boots, of a high, riding style, at first seemed black patent leather, but when viewed peripherally came alive with shifting color. On his chest was a black nameplate on which a word was spelled out in blocky red disconnected lights:

*RATAXES.*

In his first survey he had taken in Meg with the furniture, eyes hesitating only a flicker as he noted her presence. Having completed his three-sixty, however, he immediately turned on his heel and advanced until he stood over her. Without a word he reached down, grasped her covers and flipped them back. Whimpering, she brought up her arms to cover her naked breasts. She drew up her legs, rolled so that she presented her back to him, tightened her curl, forced out a broken, "Please."

The man snorted.

"So," he said, "You are the next subject of the spinners' scheme for eugenic conquest."

He reached down and fingered a lock of her hair, then touched her cheek with the backs of his fingers. She pulled away. He took a step back, snorted again.

"If you'll do for their brood sow, you'll serve as well for mine. I have need of many heirs."

He began to unbutton his tunic.

At that moment the front door banged open, admitting a fast moving body that slammed into the opposite wall, changed direction, and rocketed into Meg's bedroom to resolve as Jack, dancing around the man with a boxer's shuffle, throwing jabs at the air with such speed that the motion of his arm was difficult to follow.

"Well, little spinner..." the man began, but Jack cut him off by darting behind and pounding his kidneys with a blur of right-left combinations. The man stumbled and paled.

"Take that, you skinnerd!" Jack yelled, skipping backwards a step and feinting twice with his left.

"Little man, is she worth it?" the interloper gasped.

Jack responded by slipping back under the man's arm and popping him once in the throat with a straight left and once with a windmilling right to the solar plexus.

"Ha ha!" Jack exulted, "Hoo! Foul! Foulness! Be gone!"

The soldier staggered back against the chest that held Meg's clothing.

"Damn you, spinner!" he panted. "I'll be back!"

Throwing himself forward, he whirled on one heel. With a deafening clap, a series of blue lightning-like flashes and the smell of ozone, he was gone.

Thrm'm poured into the room, clustered around a sobbing Meg and set to work stroking, caressing, massaging her, bathing her in soothing song.

"He's gone now," Jack said, his chest heaving and his face cherry red from exertion. "Nothing to fear. He's gone."

Meg rolled over to face him.

"Who was that? How did he get here?"

"Well, um, that..." Jack hesitated, hiding a cough behind his hand. He sniffed, managing to convey a wordless suggestion of distaste before continuing less subtly, "That was the General. A real sleazy sort of rat bastard, excuse my French."

"General of what? How did he get here?"

"He's, ah, he's kind of a self-made general," Jack said, reluctance lingering in his voice. "That is, he's general of his own army, his own personal army. An army of his own person, even. You know, a little knowledge is dangerous?"

"Why don't you answer me?" Meg pleaded. "How did he get here? Where did he come from? Can he come back?"

Jack stared, Meg thought, at her breasts. But when she had covered herself and his gaze still never wavered she realized that whatever he was seeing was in the thoughts grinding away in his head. He exhaled noisily and shook himself, then jammed his hand deep into the bag he carried, rummaging for a moment before producing a small pouch. The contents of this he emptied rattling into his hand, which he closed and began to shake. He let fly and three black dice pocked onto the blanket beside her leg. She assumed they were the same he had used before. Two of them were octahedrons inscribed on their faces with white symbols. The third was a cube that looked to be mostly blank. She saw a symbol on one face turned part way toward her.

"Full Moon and Starburst!" Jack exclaimed. "Guidance I ask for and Nod counsels Strength." He chuckled. "Probably it's telling me I've got all the strength I need to put my foot in it really deep."

"If you know what's going on, if you know anything, please," her voice dwindled as she tried to prevent it from breaking with emotion, "tell me."

"You know what's going to happen," Jack answered. "I'm going to end up having to explain everything, and it'll be my explanation instead of Cousin's, and she'll come down on me for the world that comes out of the way you go left when I go right at all the things I've got no idea how to properly say. But, what the hell, right? Sometimes you just have to shake the pillars for the whole house of cards, right? Whatever's going to happen is going to happen." He paused, weighing this statement, then added as an afterthought, "Right?"

He took a deep breath before he continued.

"No, I don't think that he can come back."

With great vigor, he shook his head as he said this. Meg almost thought she heard it rattle. But once determined to talk, he launched in without further preliminary.

"Cousin Kate, Ekaterina, she says his control's not all that good. How he got here's probably coincidence. Probably picked up on the dimensional turbulence our jumps caused in interstitial being or something, you know, some crap like that. Recognized something in the interference pattern as home reality—even if the time was off—and dove into the thick of it. To even find us he'd have to dive exactly back, time for time, space for space, which is pretty high flight 'pataphysical, and he's got no 'pataphysics at all. And just the bare bones of metamathemagics, at that. You know, just the four basic functions: extending, condensing, narratizing and guesswork. Not even enough to jump."

Despite her lingering weakness and fatigue, and in spite of her abated but also lingering fear, Meg was intrigued.

"Wasn't that a jump when he disappeared?"

"Um. No." Jack said flatly. "Not really."

He squinted, and appeared to reconsider this denial, then amended, "At least, not what we think of as a jump. Not a bona fide cross-consensual leap through, or over, or under for that matter, or even around the boundaries of realized, uh, whatcha-callit? Opinion."

"But what was it he did, then?" she challenged. "Where did he go?"

"That faker. He doesn't know squat about consensa." Jack's face screwed up in a grimace that was equal parts disappoint-ment and disdain. "He only found us this time because he just happened to be at a time and a place where the ramifications of our jumps to save you washed over, set up resonances he could detect. Coincidence. Coincidence."

As he said this Jack flicked his hands. To Meg it looked as though he was trying to shake something off and away.

"That skinnerd don't jump," he continued. "Couldn't. Can't. Jump requires a basic kind of oneness-with-all type of thing, sur-render of self, that whole shebang. It's, ah, how do you say it? Incompatible? Yes, incompatible with power lust. And power, sweet friend o' mine, is what the general is all about. World-you-better-believe-it-Conquest."

"That's what he said about you," Meg retorted.

"Of course he's going to say that," Jack answered "What else is he going to say? He thinks everybody wants power. The consensual frontier is opaque to him, impervious. A wall he doesn't even know confines him."

"Where did he go then?"

"A parlor trick, mere sleight of hand. Just your ordinary, every day temporal shift between parallel universes."

Meg looked at him doubtfully.

"That's not the same as what you do?" she finally asked.

"Why, botheration! No!"

Jack turned and went to the room's small window, opened it and threw wide the shutters. Through it Meg could see the golden light of high mountain morning. Patches of purple glimpsed between the wind-dancing limbs of fir and aspen told her a thunderstorm was building on the far side of a neighboring peak. Calmer, Jack again approached the bed, ready to address her question.

"All universes are conditions of matter and energy. Important stuff, I thacken, yes, but the consensa are of a...a..."

He seemed at a loss for words. His eyes darted back and forth as he strained to find the descriptions he needed. At last, his face lit up and he went on.

"Your differences in matter and energy and whatnot, now, those differences can be differences that are entire universes. See what I'm saying?" Jack flung his arms wide to illustrate the separation, his backhand catching a passing thrm full in the face, knocking the smaller being over. Jack interrupted himself to help his unintended victim from the floor, as he did so kissing the bruised forehead and apologizing to the little man. Other thrm converged tapping and warbling on their comrade as Jack picked up his line of thought.

"They could be whole other universes, but your differences of matter and energy aren't that important in finding the difference between, say, this consensus here and some other. I mean, we're talking whole entire other worlds, but maybe all the matter and energy is not only not different but maybe is the same. Exactly the same. Like it's one stuff that's in more than one way of being real. See?"

The restored thrm now approached Jack for more hugs and tapping, sounding a rapid, staccato wrr as he let his larger friend know he was neither seriously hurt nor bore a grudge. Jack scratched at the white patch in the thrm's mane under his chin and assured his 'little buddy' of his own remorse.

Meg was not sure if she "saw" Jack's explanation or not. Her head and her neck were sites of shooting pains from the effects of the general's jolt and the effort of trying to follow Jack's less than edifying talk. The rest of her body more generally ached from fever, weariness, and the drain suffered after the rush of adrenaline. Jack's murky train of thought made the little sense it did only because of the attentions of the thrm'm as they soothed, eased, and brought comfort to her shuddering form. An eddy of fresh air blew in the open window and swept the atmosphere clean of lingering rankness and carried away the dregs of the adrenaline. The tension steadily withdrew from her body under the raining touches of the Thrm.

"It's just time travel," Jack began again, patting his 'little buddy' on the back as that one moved toward the door. "And nothing special at that. He can't even shift intracosmically. It's just barnstorming."

His shoulders drooped and his head sagged. A note of regret entered his tone.

"He couldn't stick to the higher disciplines, the real rigorous stuff my cousins eat and breathe. And as for intuitive, he was, up to a point, but only so far, and that far was just not enough. He sucked up human studies right enough, though. Physics especially." The little man spoke as much to himself as to Meg. "Oh, he was sound enough on the three metamathemagical precepts, as well as the four processes. But he always wandered away from the discussions of the ancilla. You know, the real juice. Just like he was intuitive. Only he wasn't. Not enough. Didn't pay much attention to the demonstrations of the subtler rites, either."

Jack stared at the back of his hand as he spoke, but stared wasn't right because his eyes weren't really focused. He seemed profoundly sad.

"As for 'pataphysics, he never showed more than a limited grasp of what it really means to be particular. Just enough to make his loops. Just enough to build his army."

Jack's attention wandered off. He fell silent.

"It sounds like you went to school together," Meg commented.

Jack's eyes darted to hers and held her fixed with his stare.

"I knew him when we both studied. Together? I don't think so." He withdrew his gaze with a dramatic roll. "Like I said, he was only so intuitive, and no more, and that wasn't enough. No, he was supposed to work at it." The dvarsh shrugged. "Instead, he learned one trick and launched this plan for conquest. Dropped the program without notice and disappeared through interstitial being. Every shift, he steps over one universe. Vacates the one where he was standing, moves into the next. But one step back in time, like an hour or a day, so he can join his parallel ownself already in progress. He convinces his parallel self, who's been thinking about it himself anyway, to join himself in this plan of conquest. Do it again, bam! there's four of them in universe number three, none in number one or two. Bam! eight in number four. Sixteen in number five. Thirty-two in six. You get the picture? See, they're, whatchacallit? converging from all these adjacent universes, leaving all those empty of generals, this particular one anyway, which is probably something. Anyway..." Jack leaned forward and patted her leg through the blanket. "...Anyway, one day, some time, somewhere down the way he expects to have a horde of himself sufficient to overwhelm some entire Podunk, backwoods cosmos. He's going to install a junta of himself, led by himself, the general, the one from universe number one, this universe, the one who started it all by being in this universe which is the universe that stands out because it's the universe where the general came earliest to his hungry conclusion and successfully devised his loop-step spatio-temporal shift style of technique. See?"

This time, Meg most certainly did not see. Even if she had been able to follow the twists of Jack's explanations, the work of the thrm'm had moved her back into something like the torpid state from which she had earlier been forced by the general's arrival. She lay passive in the stream of Jack's words, some part of her hearing key phrases, snatches, some other part of her wondering why she should trust Jack's intentions any more than Jack had thought she should trust the general's. After all, if his intentions were not honorable then it became perfectly conceivable that he, too, would lie.

But while these two parts of her worked on and on at being somewhat awake, the rest of her slipped into an approximation of light sleep, leaving her unresponsive to Jack's words. Jack didn't seem to mind. He continued for some time on the general and his plan for sometime, somewhere conquest. Meg's listening part noted several mentions of the phrase "4739th complete repeat of, you know, the full cycle, or thereabouts," which she later learned was the point in the general's impossible doubling at which the dvarsh estimated he would feel himself multiple enough to launch an attempt at conquest of a cosmos.

"One thing we think he hasn't figured on," Jack gestured emphatically, as though he had some audience other than himself, "or at least Kate thinks he hasn't figured on, but I think the same as her, you know, that is, I agree, like I'd be a fool not to, is that army of ten gazillion stone cold, heartless sons-o-burning-breeches, each one has his identical ambition, see? Because an infinite number is one whole big bunch of universes but it's all just one consensus. See what I mean?"

He underscored this with a nod and a wink toward unresponsive Meg.

"Looks to me," Jack concluded, "like number one has overlooked the fact that he's in the way of his own advancement ten gazillion times over. And now he's darting off on solo side trips wanting who knows what. Call it only a matter of time before that train pulls into Coup d'Etat City."

Jack favored his uncaring companion with a beatific grin.

"What a noise he'll be making then."

# Eleven

MEG OPENED HER EYES TO THE sound of Jack's snores and the lisping breath of the dozens of sleeping creatures in each of the cabin's two rooms. Her bladder felt near to bursting. She was naked except for the diaper-like cloth in which someone—Jack, she presumed, or the little people—had dressed her, but her thick terry cloth robe hung from a hook in the wall above the head of her cot. She knew that she had been wetting herself for some untold number of days, and that she was still dressed in the diaper because she was expected to wet herself again.

"But not anymore," she promised herself.

She was recovered enough to be sharply aware of the sweat-and-urine crust to the sheets between which she lay, knew that she had soiled them once since the one fresh change she remembered. The first step to replacing them with clean was getting up, and no reason better for getting up than to stop wetting her bed and start using the privy again like, she told herself, like a human, or like...what...?"

She let that thought dangle.

Her groping for the robe roused Sweetheart, who sat up, eyes wide, and uttered a breathy interrogative chirrup.

"I've got to pee," Meg said softly, and the small being replied with a series of rapid, barely audible clucks.

Robe in hand, Meg swung her legs off the cot and sat up in one motion. She was rocked by a tidal wave of dizziness and nausea. Letting her head and upper body sag as far forward as her full bladder would allow, she waited for her stomach to go back down her throat and her head to clear. Awkwardly, she slipped her arms into her robe as she maintained this position.

She was breathing in rapid, shallow pants when she felt the pressure of small hands on her temples. Opening her eyes she found Sweetheart standing directly before her, sympathetic tears brimming in liquid eyes, her oddly formed little hands pressing ever so slightly on the sides of Meg's head. Strangely, it helped. Whatever Jack's intentions, she felt no threat from these diminutive people-things. Their every gesture, particularly Sweetheart's, had been to bring her ease from pain. Whatever they were, whatever they turned out to be, she was certain that she owed them her life.

A groping foot located her shoes, the scuffed loafers she liked to wear around the cabin. Slipping them on she began slowly to stand, steadying herself with a hand to the wall. Weaker than she had ever known herself, she found standing nearly more than she could manage. Fog closed in on her and the room began to dip crazily, but she forced the feeling to pass and her vision cleared. Sweetheart looked on nervously, swaying a little but making no sound. When Meg was stably upright the smaller being darted to her side, grabbed Meg's hand and placed it on her—Sweetheart's—head. She held it there and braced herself in a way that told Meg she was expected to lean down on that head for support. One of the sticks these people carried would have worked better, but she could never have leaned over to pick it up, and by now she was desperate to urinate.

This camp, unlike any other run by the agency that employed her, held two structures, not counting the outhouse. At other stations the living space was in the tower, which was larger, roomier than the crow's perch that served here. No other watch camp was as high, or as remote from the base office. The two room cabin, a spacious accommodation compared to other sites, and the smaller tower were the products of a long past eccentric private effort to police for fires. When the agency had assumed jurisdiction it had absorbed this high camp as it stood, the individuals involved glad enough not to pack construction materials to that far quarter that they felt no qualms about deviating from specifics of mandated watch camp standards.

When Meg and Mr. Christmas had come to this work after Meg's mother had died, this site above all others had seemed perfectly suited for the two of them. However, the relative spaciousness now meant she had to cross through the cabin, weaving among sleeping thrm'm, and circle around it outside to the booth that housed their comfort station. At least, she reminded herself, she did not have to negotiate the ladder-like stairs that led down from the all-in-one tower residences of other camps.

The walk to the outhouse was excruciating, but she made it, worried the whole way that she would stumble and snap Sweetheart's neck. But the creature seemed unfazed. At the door to the outhouse Sweetheart was persistent in trying to come in with her, but Meg mustered the firmness to hold her out while getting a grip on the door. Alone at last, in the close darkness of the rough wood compartment, she hiked her robe, shoved down her diaper, perched and peed buckets.

The very sense of relief was draining. Having finished she sat for several minutes, not wanting to move, wondering what else was in store for her.

Inside her cabin a strange man rambled on and on in an almost but not quite incoherent way. He claimed her father was dead and that she was sick from a disease caused by listening to news of a war on the radio. He told her this troop of creatures so suddenly all around her was a kind of elf tribe who intended to make her pregnant after they healed her so they could "take back" the world.

"Is this," she asked herself, "a reasonable story?"

Besides, she reasoned, even apart from his hint of plans for her, he seemed awfully preoccupied with sex.

And there were those other...incidents, the ones of which he denied any knowledge. She was pretty sure they were more than just dreams.

Yet even if Jack were not a threat, there was that other one, the general who said he would rape her, and said he would be back. To trust Jack's word that the general could not return meant that she had to trust Jack, at least a little. There was something, maybe even a lot of things, about the weird little man that she felt drawn to like, but trust? Struggling in the olid darkness of the rude two-holer, to be candid with herself—to be, in the term she silently assigned, level-headed—she had to acknowledge there were things about Jack she could understand only in terms of perversion.

She decided she was in serious trouble.

Under different circumstances she would have allowed herself to be too weak to stand. But now, what she needed to do was get away, and since she had already left the cabin without raising an alarm this was probably the best opportunity she would have. True, she was only wearing loafers, a soiled diaper, and a long terry cloth robe but to change clothes would mean going back inside, and that would surely give her away. The next station was a day's hike away for a healthy person, but to stay here and become breeding stock for Jack's vague genetic invasion was not her idea of an option.

"Now or never," she told herself.

Opening the door at first a crack, she expected to see Sweetheart waiting close by to aid her. But Sweetheart was not in her line of sight. Opening the door wider and sticking her head out, she reconnoitered. For a moment she saw nothing. Then she sensed movement at the edge of the clearing in which the cabin sat, a nearly silent commotion under the fronds of some large ferns, which a long stare finally resolved into Sweetheart and one of the elf-men, copulating vigorously, their skirts and shawls hiked up and tangled, but without their calls, the ragged in and out of their breathing the only sounds they made. In spite of herself Meg felt a little betrayed, but also grateful. Just when she needed her caregiver's attention distracted a distraction was provided. They were even at a point on the clearing's edge, which had no view of the trail down, that being blocked by the cabin. Meg forced herself to move quickly, one foot in front of the other, crossed the clearing and started down the trail.

She had walked for about fifteen minutes when she heard a snuffling, grunting, scraping commotion in front of her. She stopped and put her hand out to a tree to steady herself. Her strength was draining. She had been going forward on momentum only. As her legs buckled and she sank to the foot of the tree she heard a deep, interrogative huff and watched the silhouette of a bear rise on its hind legs to block the stars from the sky over the path ahead. The bear sniffed the air then dropped to all fours and started toward her. Meg tried to rise, but could not. She gave up and waited to die. She tried to figure out whether or not it was odd the bear was awake. Despite the time she spent in their forests, she had not really given bear habits much thought. Her father had always been careful to avoid attracting them to the vicinity of their outpost. She remembered something about lying still and playing dead, but she couldn't recall if that was with bear or cougar. There wasn't much else she could do though, collapsed against a tree, unable to move.

As the bear got closer she was unable to see it at all, so deep were the shadows. Suddenly, she felt its breath. She whimpered and cringed, shrinking from the feared attack. And then a voice beside her was saying, "Shoo, shoo, shoo." She heard the repetitive hissing wheeze of some device and felt the cool drift of mist onto her hand. The bear bawled and seemed to roll over and away from her, bawled again and thrashed the bushes, then— from the sound—departed at a gallop, bawling and trumpeting in anger and pain.

"Such a sick young woman to be out in these woods," said the voice, a deep, throaty female voice. "Alone and defenseless. I wouldn't step into these woods without my trusty spray can. Oh, dear, child, now, yes, go ahead and faint..."

# *Twelve*

## ))

MEG REGAINED CONSCIOUSNESS BACK ON THE cot. She knew immediately that the sheets were clean and so was she. Jack's voice, low and droning, drifted around her.

"Before long you'll come up on the limitation of planets, and we're looking forward to that with a mix of hope and trepidation. Maybe it'll shock you into renouncing the acquisitive fallacy, maybe not. Could be you'll just turn your greedy hands across the consensual planes. Ha, ha! Could be you'll become an even nastier threat to us than now."

Jack mumbled as he fidgeted with items on the rude chest that held Meg's possessions. He stood against the light of the open window, a dark shape relieved by a little color around the edges. A fresh breeze rustled those curls of his hair and beard visible like a nimbus around his silhouetted head, and carried an evergreen scent to the sickbed. The tone of his voice was mumble enough, but the actual volume at which he spoke suggested he did not mind if these perhaps not entirely random thoughts were overheard.

"Jackanapes, it could be that you'll stop with that carrying on and be properly pleased to see your cousin just returned."

The woman who spoke these words was slightly shorter than Jack and leaner, more compact. And broader. It was surprising to Meg just how broad, especially since the woman was not in the least thick from back to front. Her skin, where it was exposed on her face, a bit of neck, her hands, had the color of an unsmoked briar. Despite differences, Meg thought the woman similar enough to Jack to confirm the suggested kinship. Even so, that peculiar man did seem like a mixture of gene sources in comparison, and this woman in the doorway to the room looked like the pure fruit of what could only be the dvarsh line. The extraordinary breadth combined with the obvious leanness, even sleekness, of muscle, much more pronounced in her than in Jack, indicated a distinctly non-human origin.

She turned directly to the girl on the cot.

"I am Ekaterina Rigidstick, of the Nondifferential Clan, a people of the nation called Dvarsh. I am pleased to see you recovered to the extent I might find you walking around the mountain. We did so worry for a time we would lose you."

"Where did you come from?" Meg asked. She caught herself checking the atmosphere for any whiff of ozone.

"The question should properly be how did you two—or, at least, he—remain unaware of me from my first probe two days ago until now. And the answer, I suspect, is that you, Jackanapes, were not paying attention. Which says quite a bit in itself. You should know better."

She glared at Jack, whose head sank down on his shoulders like a chastened puppy.

"Why don't you stow the new supplies before our friends scatter them everywhere in their abandon."

Jack rose to leave. As Ekaterina moved into the room to let him pass, Meg gasped in amazement. Through the doorway she saw the other room dense with elves grappling in procreative frenzy. Strangely quiet, they gave voice to little more than faint clicks and pants. They all, male and female, had their skirts hiked up above the waist, and their shawls open exposing their chests. They joined with rapt attention, rolling occasionally so that now one was up, now the other, their hands and feet moving constantly to touch each his or her partner over every part of the body.

"Like the frieze on a Hindu ruin..." Ekaterina's voice trailed off, then she added, "They have to return to this consensus in order to conceive. They're taking advantage of the opportunity. We don't get them here so often any more..."

"I think Jack said something about that. I thought you, I mean the one's like you, the...," Meg's voice dropped slightly, "dwarves, have to do that also."

"Yes. Exactly so." Ekaterina clapped her hands together as though dusting them off. "But you and I have other subjects to discuss, Patricia Margaret Christmas. So, let us get off on the proper footing. I suppose you have the typical human name-shame that compels you to use a shortened form. Would it be 'Patricia,' 'Margaret,' 'Pat'...,"

"Meg?"

"What's that?"

"Meg. I go by 'Meg.'"

The dvarsh woman inclined her head very slightly.

"Meg, then."

She moved to assume Jack's seat, folding her hands onto her lap as she arranged herself on the ladderback, her feet several inches off the floor.

"Now. Where did Jackanapes leave off?"

She leaned forward as she spoke, her eyes swimming with reflected light and a warm intensity. Her expression was expectant.

"Leave off?"

Meg thought for a moment she might be alluding to Jack's questionable activities.

"With whatever garble he was filling your head full of." Ekaterina smiled, only a little archly. "Notions of which you should believe no more than half."

"Well..."

Meg looked back into those eyes. Here, her heart told her, was someone on whom she could rely.

"I...I'd decided there was a good chance he's crazy. It wasn't just the things he said. I was thinking he was maybe some kind of..." she groped for a word, "weirdo? I was trying to get away while he was sleeping. He never hurt me, but it's all been kind of scary. I couldn't tell if I could count on him, and the things he said were so strange."

Meg's gaze skirted timidly just above the end of Ekaterina's shoulder, dancing like gnats in the airy space.

"Very good, dear," said Ekaterina, punctuating her comments with vigorous nodding. The gesture immediately reminded Meg of the way Jack seemed to accompany everything he said with a nodding or shaking of his head. "Direct and truthful. Your fever breaks, you wake up to a house full of the dear ones and a strange man with strange words and a strange manner tells you that your father is dead and you are direly ill a hard day's march from another human. Something like that?"

"Yes."

"What else? As I know Jackanapes he would not be content with only that."

Ekaterina was once more leaning forward, head cocked with hands on her knees.

"That you were going to take over the world and part of the way you're going to do it is by...by," again Meg's voice dropped, following the cast of her eyes toward the floor, "making me have a baby."

Meg looked sharply and defiantly into Ekaterina's eyes. The older woman was quick to speak.

"Neither characterization is correct, although I can certainly see how you would get to that from my cousin's potential for scrambling explanations. A great poet, yes, all agree, but no prose." Here Ekaterina mimicked her cousin again by slowly, broadly shaking her head. "Rest easy on that count, child. None of us," she placed a very subtle stress on the pronoun, "is going to make you do a single thing you don't want to do. Our only priority at this time is getting you once more hale and strong. Maybe later you'll take an interest in what we're trying to accomplish in the larger arena."

Relief showed on the young woman's face.

Suddenly Jack burst in, assumed his declamative posture and began:

> "I commit myself. A Babylonian, overwrought
> and anguished with lust for his lady—the moon,
>     Luna,
> Astarte, some kind of goddess or tart
> or another, just out of reach, long distance,
> a crap shoot if ever there was one, dear hearts—
> this pilgrim besat himself as on a train,
> riding the planet like he would the club car
> at night, in the rain, in a strange country.
> His cigarette, forgotten, ready to char
> within a smidgen of blistering his careless fingers
> that make indolent gestures before him in the air
> in the crude form of half-forgotten acts of worship,

*he did, or would have except, by Marduk's gar,*
*Babylon had a twig or two, some terraces,*
*the pimped up limestone shack of Nubble K' Neezar,*
*but not once, even briefly, a railroad.*
*Attend, for so speak the gods,*
*and any one of them can kick your ass."*

Jack stood with his hand on his breast while Ekaterina applauded and called "Bravo!" several times.

Meg was surprised by the other woman's enthusiasm.

"Do you really think his poems are any good?" she asked.

"I'm sure they are great," Ekaterina answered. "He works so hard at them and his intentions are quite artistic. On the strength of quantity of output alone he ranks among the most prodigious bards of the Dvarsh. And as you have just heard, he can also be quite modern "

Meg thought about this a long moment before speaking again.

"Are there lots of poets among the Dvarsh?" she asked, somewhat tentatively.

"Well, no, actually," Ekaterina admitted, "Not that many. And all of them have had at least a trace of human blood. We have meditated on this a great deal. Pureblood Dvarsh seem to lack a crucial faculty for garbling concepts and phraseology. I've set out several times to make a poem only to discover that I was writing a report or preparing a list or, once, observing and cataloging every measurable dimension of a location in which I had been both touched and moved by witnessing an act of perfectly selfless generosity. Which does not mean, however, that there is not a distinctly dvarsh cast to the lyrics and lays of our bards. I especially like how you don't have to listen to the sense of the words, how they can just sort of be around one like a pleasant background while one thinks of something else—and if it is a very good poem nothing about it will jar one or interrupt one's thoughts."

"Oh," said Meg. "I've been trying to figure out what he means."

"Oh, dear Gussie," said Ekaterina, "don't do that, child. You'll suffer a relapse. Poetry should be taken as a piece of the environment that one endures because it probably has some, ah, elements that contribute in some fashion to the general uplift of culture."

Ekaterina smiled weakly.

"Isn't that kind of like ignoring it?" Meg asked.

"Yes, but ignoring it without withdrawing approval."

The dvarsh slapped her leg and winked as she said this.

The younger woman pressed her question, "Does that mean you get a goofy expression on your face while your mind's a million miles away?"

"That's only part of it. Approval takes an active form. We give them grants and fellowships and awards, and funding so they can throw an occasional banquet. One of them gets to say something at any public ceremony we have."

"Does that seem like enough for them? For all their work?"

The young woman's brows knit incredulously.

"Meg, dear, we're talking about poets. It's not like they spend their lives thinking about reasonable or important things, you know."

"Hah!" burst out Jack, who had until that moment listened to the exchange as though it were a continuing ovation for his performance. "Not true, not true. I comment on matters of great moment...," he paused as he drew himself erect, "...whenever commissioned."

"I see what you mean," Meg observed to Ekaterina.

"Oh, Cousin," Jack broke in. "I forgot."

"Forgot what, dear boy?"

"I forgot the general paid a visit. Scared the pee out of the girl."

"Rataxes! Here? How did you greet him?"

"With a whack and a smack and a bam, bam, bam!"

Jack pantomimed these acts as he named them. Ekaterina flushed an even darker hue.

"Jackanapes, I'm warning you. If you keep on like this you are going to provoke a real hostility in that man."

"He was going to slip it to our human! Had her sheets down and was starting to remove his costume. It called for fast action!"

Jack barked his red-faced protest with arms thrown wide.

"Is this accurate?"

Ekaterina turned to Meg.

"Yes," Meg answered, her own face grown pale behind a grimly set jaw. "That was another reason I wanted to get away from here."

Ekaterina looked thoughtful for a moment, then said, "Okay, Jackanapes. You did as you needed."

Jack, validated and on a poet's high, bounded out of the room.

Ekaterina stared into space.

# *Thirteen*

After Jack's departure Ekaterina seemed lost in thought. Meg had not been inclined to break the silence between them while the older woman still showed the stress of some internal conflict in her bearing. After a few minutes, Ekaterina took spinning materials from her bag and began to spin.

Unlike Jack, she used a drop spindle and distaff, and unlike Jack she produced a fine thread of uniform quality.

Within a heartbeat of having taken up this activity the tension seemed to leave her, an ease coming into her carriage as she established the regular motion of her work. Meg found herself nearly hypnotized by the metrical drop, spin and take up of new thread. With a start she realized that she had lost track of passing time. She shook her head once to clear it, and all the strangeness, all the difficult questions she had set aside came back to her.

"Can I ask you about some of the things that Jack was saying? About something you said?"

Only reluctantly did Meg interrupt the quiet that had fallen between the two of them. She found the spinning nearly as soothing to watch as the other found it to do. Words, she feared, might detract from its effect. Nevertheless, the older woman responded without hesitation.

"Oh, absolutely."

Ekaterina's hands continued unbroken in the rhythm of her craft.

"I don't understand what you mean when you say 'consensus.' I mean, sometimes it was like Jack was telling me that you live on another world, but then it's almost like this other world isn't another place, but just a...a big..." She felt frustration grow at her difficulty finding language for the shape of her thoughts, "...complicated...difference of...opinion?"

Ekaterina broke into a broad smile.

"You are every bit as promising as we thought when we caught your vibrations. What you just said is more or less correct, both 'pataphysically and psychologically. Although the mathemagics are somewhat more complex than your elegant summation implies. Our worlds are, indeed, we have discovered, physical opinions. To a certain extent you're just going to have to take that on faith. Some of your scientists are beginning to feel the tickle of the first inkling. Another twenty generations, if they live, and humankind will be jumping the consensa as readily as do the dvarsh."

"You lost me," Meg said. "At least, I think you did. I mean, I understand all of the words, but all together they make something I just don't see."

She exhaled loudly, abruptly, then went on, "I mean, you live on another world, but it's not another planet."

"In," Ekaterina corrected her, "It would be more accurate to say that we live 'in' another world rather than 'on.'"

"Okay." Meg nodded her head as she mulled the distinction. She then continued, "You live there, but you have to come here to conceive, which you do by 'jumping,'" she was careful to pronounce the word as if with quotes, "which I suppose means something other than hopping up and down." This image seemed to arrest her thought. She paused and blinked it away, then went on. "And you come here with these creatures you call 'thrm'm' but say that these are what we mean when we say 'elves.' And the thrm'm are sort of like people but with weird hands and extra senses and no eg...eg...oh, what was it Jack said...eggle-conscience?"

"Ego-consciousness?" the other prompted.

"That's it!"

"Jackanapes said that?"

"He said it was a quote."

Ekaterina seemed to swell a little, and her face took on the slightest cast of self-satisfaction.

"At least the dear boy gives credit, even if text and understanding are some decades superceded."

"Yes, ma'am. Anyway," a flush rose slowly in Meg's cheeks as her spirits began to stir with her subject, "they don't have it like we do, and they don't talk but they have this strong desire..."

"An instinct, dear."

"An instinct to take care of sick people."

As she spoke, Meg seemed to accumulate tension as quickly as Ekaterina had shed it. Ekaterina appeared deliberately not to notice.

"Yes. What else?"

"Well. There's you and Jack. You talk about things in really, really, um...unusual? ways, and you aren't quite shaped like other people. You talk about coming here by following vibrations," Meg's hands clenched into white knuckled fists as she talked, her brow knit, "and sending beams to each other and jumping, and my dad's dead and I nearly died..." Her voice took on a quaver as her whole body drew taut. Emotions she had not even known she harbored pushed their way out through her words. "But I'm getting better by...by...by nursing from Sweetheart and all those...those elves...are... in the other room there...doing...THAT, and I don't understand why you're here and why you know so much about me unless...unless...."

"Unless we want you for something?" Ekaterina offered in her same bright, kindly accents.

"Yes," the young woman agreed grimly, "Unless you want me for something."

Meg had been on the verge of being overwhelmed by rising anger. She had started simply to summarize whatever she could identify as real or alleged facts, but as she had talked the flood of fears and feelings dammed inside had welled and threatened to burst. She stared at Ekaterina, struggling to get herself under control and trying to make her expression something like confident determination.

"After all," she burst out, "what makes you so different from that general?"

"Meg, my child, I'm afraid my cousin Jackanapes may have led you to develop a somewhat erroneous notion of our aims. We shall not force you to do anything. We are asking you, indeed, imploring you to help us."

Ekaterina spoke from a rocker she had produced out of those mysterious precincts she called her exilic home, a rocker sized for a person of her shape and height. Between one glance from the sickbed and another, she had brought it to replace the narrow ladderback that had been Jack's roost in the sick room. There had been no disturbance, nothing that interrupted Meg's account. The younger woman looked away from the elder seated uneasily on an ill-proportioned chair, and looked back to find her ensconced in a piece scaled to her frame. Ekaterina's feet were now firmly grounded as she rocked slowly in time with the sure movements of her hands.

"You want me to help you take over the world?" Meg stared at her, disbelieving her eyes as much as she disbelieved a genuine plea for help to change the world would ever come to her, would ever come to anyone, really.

"Dear Meg," the dvarsh spoke so softly the younger woman had difficulty hearing. "We came, most importantly, because we wanted to save you. With no strings attached. We came because who you are, how you are, is precious in this world. A light that cannot be allowed to dim. We hoped to save your father as well, but we were too late. He was too far gone into the fever..." she sat up straight and her voice grew stronger, "But, yes, we are hoping you will agree to something we will ask you to do."

Meg could feel fear edging back in. She had hoped that raising aloud the question of their intentions would elicit denial of any ulterior plans for her and protestations of dwarfish and elfish altruism. She looked out through the window at the branches of spruce waving in a breath of wind. It now hung between them—if, as she was told, she was being healed for the healing, somewhere on the other side of that gift lurked the possibility of another agenda. Her voice cracked when she asked the obvious.

"What...what do you want me to do?"

"Sweet Meg. We don't want you to do anything that you don't feel right about. We do want to ask you for help, and in a big way. We want to ask you for a commitment that will last for decades. It will be your choice to say yes or no." Ekaterina gave her a look that underscored this assertion. "Say no and we will be disappointed, but we will understand."

"And if I say yes?"

"Then you will join us in our vast and desperate transconsensidimensional struggle."

"What..."

Meg almost whispered the word, stopping as her mouth went dry. Resisting the question she was trying to press, her tongue grew thick and numb.

"What...," she began again and stopped, drawing air deep into her lungs. She swallowed hard.

She let the word float through her. Its meaning held neither hot nor cold on her thoughts. She lowered her head slightly, keeping her eyes locked on Ekaterina, and repeated...

"What...," the pent up breath came out almost a sigh, "do you want me to do?"

"Well," Ekaterina looked straight into the young human's eyes, "We would, indeed, like you to have a baby."

# *Fourteen*

"WE LOOKED AT THE EMERGING WORLDVIEWS among humans on the Eurasian landmass, and the religions growing up around those worldviews. It didn't seem to make much difference which version you considered, things looked bad. The sense of being of the earth was disappearing and this displacement was shaping development of human technology and its applications."

Meg's reaction to the proposal that she have a baby sent her to the verge of panic. Sweetheart had voiced an aria of twitters, trills, coos, and chirps, which she accompanied by a whispering cascade of glancing, nearly-not touches over the young woman's body, and, in response, Meg calmed. Still she kept her eyes away from Ekaterina, despite the fascinating quickness with which the older woman turned fiber to thread. Ekaterina, for her part, talked on, knowing the human was listening, even if she did not reply.

Meg absently stroked Sweetheart under a shoulder blade with an index finger. The thrm had slipped down and was half-sitting, half-laying against Meg, apparently in a light doze.

"We dvarsh were increasingly subjected to horrible brutalities in every contact with no longer communing humans. The Eurasian populations were ever more engaged in crushing the way of clans and tribes not only among themselves, but wherever they found it. It was like a great sickness infecting your species, and a strain of it even took hold in parts of these two isolated continents long before the Eurasian invasions. The human clans and tribes were crushed by the rise of your cities before you could adapt those structures as we did. The rise of armies replaced the moral discipline of the warrior with the immoral one of the mercenary soldier. How awful to pay and be paid for killing your own, yet life in one's own filth and refuse became a kind of unquestioned banner of 'progress' for humans. The uses your people made of thrm'm were unspeakable." She shook her head and went on. "We gathered the Thrm and took them to havens in these Americas, Australia, or remote corners of Africa that had not succumbed to the madness. Also to some of the islands of the sea. We continued to mix with many of the aborigines of the Americas, the islanders of the Pacific, Australia's original habitants, some African peoples south of the Living Desert. We also kept genetically mixed agents working to maintain a spark of the loving way in even the darkest citadels of Eurasia. It was apparent to us that this darkness would be something that would have to play out. We would have to live through it, and it might prevail. And, in that event, all, ALL, would be lost. It was, and is, our place to struggle, and to give tongue and form to the loving way."

She paused to work a snarl from her fiber. Deft fingers released it in a blink.

"Approximately four thousand years ago our meditations and study led us to discover the manifold nature of being, the fact that all possibilities are. We developed the disciplines that allow us to move through all the consensa as birds move through the air, with will, volition. Not randomly and in ignorance as humans do now and as we did before." Ekaterina glanced sidewise at the younger woman and caught her peeking back. "'Consensa' is how we translate to your tongue our word for the paths that flow through possibility, and there is much to it that we do not even in four millennia understand. But we do know that beings have an inseverable tie to the consensus from which they arise." Her eyes came to rest on her recalcitrant listener. "A consensus is not any given set of specific possibilities, but rather a path in which the possibilities are continuous and in certain ways self-consistent." She paused, as for a breath, letting this statement sink in. "It is the ultimate enforcement of responsibility that if you abandon your natal consensus you abandon your capability for procreation. Nevertheless," the dvarsh drew herself even more erect, "the disciplines allow us to base our struggle to save our home in discrete, but more or less proximate, possible realities. The disciplines of moving through the consensa give us our only advantage in the struggle to keep the loving way alive."

Ekaterina stopped when the younger woman suddenly looked straight into her eyes.

"You're talking about magic!" Meg exclaimed.

In spite of herself she was drawn to the story the dvarsh was unfolding. She now looked steadily at Ekaterina, although her unconscious finger still caressed Sweetheart's back.

"Well, yes. 'Magic' is one of the terms humans have used for certain of our disciplines. It has been used especially by those who have sought to identify and destroy our practitioners, and by those who have sought knowledge of our practices out of hope of turning them to personal gain. For us it is life practice, discipline, as are our meditations and our addresses to Ultimate Being."

"Ultimate Being?" Something about that term brought Meg's attention fully to bear. She sensed that it related to ideas she had herself tried to make sensible. "Is that like God?"

"God," Ekaterina said explosively, then blew noisily through pursed lips. She turned to gaze out the window, her hands freezing in mid labor. Meg was on the verge of breaking the silence when Ekaterina's hands began again to spin and her eyes turned back to meet the human's.

"The notion of 'God' is at the shallowest level of understanding. For most humans it is completely misdirected, a complete misconception." Her brow furrowed as she sought to make her point clear. "A child's way of thinking pinned to the unutterably selfish fantasy of personal redemption or salvation or relief or exaltation—depending on the permutation you want to discuss. And these, you must know, are dire perversities."

The dvarsh woman shuddered at the images these words provoked for her.

"It's wrong to want to be saved?" Meg was pulling herself into a more upright position, increasingly excited by this turn of subject.

"Child, you are still not fully recovered, you must take care," Ekaterina admonished.

"Yes, ma'am. I mean, I will, Ekaterina. But besides that, is it wrong to want to be saved?"

Meg was trembling, almost unable to contain herself. Sweetheart sat up abruptly and began to minister to her, but

Meg grabbed the other's hands and patted them as a way of showing she was not distressed.

Ekaterina spoke slowly and with tremendous gravity, a precise gap after each precisely uttered word.

"There is no more wicked vanity."

"What about the desire for corporeal immortality?" Jack asked, sitting up suddenly on the floor beside Meg's cot, causing her to jerk back and gasp. "Or even just artificial lengthening of a mostly wasted mortal life?"

"Jackanapes! That is absolutely no way either to announce yourself or to join a conversation," Ekaterina fumed at him. "If you don't come in by the door you must give signs or a warning. You could scare a body to death."

"Right, I get you," he acknowledged. "But what about what I said? You know, corporeal immortality is a pretty wicked idea, too. Isn't it?"

"Yes. Okay. The desire for personal salvation is one of the wickedest vanities," Ekaterina amended.

"I knew it!" Meg cried, flushing with a triumph that mimicked her fever. "After my mother died my father used to let my grandmother take me to church. Gran used to say that some people loved God because they were afraid of going to hell if they didn't, and that that wasn't really loving God. She said she loved God because he offered us salvation and that that was true love, but it seemed just the same thing to me. It was still just like you were loving God because you got something out of it. I've always thought that if you really love God you wouldn't be thinking at all about yourself but just loving him because, you know, he just...he just deserves it."

"Or she," Jack chided, wagging a finger, "Or she deserves it."

Ekaterina said nothing for a moment, looking at Meg from behind a wide-eyed hint of tears. At last she spoke.

"We suspected this when we caught the timbre of your vibrations and determined the nature of your illness. You are wise beyond your years." She affirmed this statement with a single, slow nod. "You really do show great promise."

Meg sobered.

"You mean great promise for having a baby?" she shot back.

Ekaterina allowed herself a slight upturning at the corners of her mouth in a passing suggestion of a smile.

"For that, yes. And for...other things."

"You're close," said Jack, "But not quite right on. It's not like an eye can love the person it's part of. See what I'm saying?"

The two women ignored him. He stood up and dusted off the seat of his pants.

"What kind of other things?" Meg asked.

"But not an eye like a person's eye, either." Jack, noting he had the attention of neither, continued undeterred. "More something like a scallop's eye, you know? Like one of a multitude. Each sees something, but only what all see together is the something seen. See?"

Jack ambled across the room, stopped in the doorway, turned and looked back at the two women still fixed on each other, still paying him no mind.

"If you agree to our proposal, we, that is, Jackanapes and I, will teach you the basics of the disciplines," Ekaterina told Meg.

"Only everything possible to see," Jack said, "is another scallop's eye, seeing what it's possible for a scallop's eye to see. All the eyes together make some kind of picture of a scallop's knowing. At least about scallops. More or less."

Having said this, he turned again and walked out of the room.

Ekaterina's proposal still floated in the air between the two women. Neither said anything for several minutes as Meg tried to take in what this meant for her. The quiet between them went on for so long that she gradually became aware of the soft calls and constant rustling of many elves in the adjacent room, as well as a low repetitive grunting that could only be Jack.

"What are they doing in there?" she asked.

"Mating. Furiously."

"Still?" Meg asked incredulously.

The dvarsh smiled.

"I told you that they, and we, must come back to our home consensus to conceive. It's a rare opportunity to be able to bring so many at one time to a safe place."

"Jack, too?"

Ekaterina threw back her head and laughed.

"Yes, him, too. He truly does have thrm'mic blood, you know. He's quite a spectacular hybrid."

Meg nodded solemnly behind a blush.

"What are those dice he gets out sometimes?" She covered embarrassment by changing the subject. "The ones he uses when he's trying to decide something."

"Oh, those," the other answered. "Those are the tokens for consulting his Nod."

"His nod?" Meg reacted with theatrical puzzlement. "What's his nod?"

But Ekaterina had already dropped her spinning to delve into her bag, from which she brought forth a small, slender volume hardbound within a well-handled mulberry fabric, and a tiny drawstring pouch in a faded version of the same color. She placed the book in Meg's hand while she opened the pouch and shook from it a set of dice like those Jack used.

The book was in Dvarsh, rendered in wholly unfamiliar but lovely script. Even so, Meg could see it consisted of some brief front matter, a series of illustrated entries and, at the back, a small number of tables and diagrams. Sprinkled in the introductory text and featured extensively in the diagrams and tables were symbols she recognized as twins to those on the dice Ekaterina now clicked in her hand. Each illustrated entry was headed by a combination of two of these symbols, various moon shapes and suns and stars and sometimes a black triangle, next to a boldface title line in Dvarsh. The illustrations of the entries seemed almost to tell a story as she flipped through the pages.

"It's beautiful," said Meg, "Especially all these drawings of clowns and dragons." Her finger traced the sinuous lines illuminating the page before her. "What does it say?"

"This," began Ekaterina as she took the book and handed over the dice for Meg's inspection, "is the ancient book of intuition of the Dvarsh. A gift to us from Nod, a heroic gynandrous clown singularity who dwelt among us millennia ago—"

"I didn't understand that," Meg broke in. "A heroic what?"

"Heroic gynandrous clown singularity," the older woman repeated. "Something like a spirit being with an indeterminate, accreted body and a terrific sense of humor. Nod organized the Guild of Intuits and taught an intuitive system called Hidden Dragon."

Ekaterina held up the book, open to a page that featured clown and beast.

"Why a dragon, though?" Meg's eyes moved from the objects in her hand back to the book the dvarsh now held. "They don't look like they fight or anything."

"Oh, no," Ekaterina answered. "Hidden Dragon is the power within each of us, within everything, of the loving way. In the loving way is the power of a hidden dragon. Nod gave us the book as an oracle of the way in our daily lives."

She turned the open leaves so she could see the exposed entry, her eyes tracing the lines of its illustrations with the affectionate gaze of long familiarity.

"We call it Nod's Way." She closed the covers and folded her hands around it. "Or sometimes simply Nod. In a sense we identify the book with the departed donor. Through the use of the oracle we can each come to know and grow close to our ancestral friend."

"But Jack doesn't use the book," Meg objected. "He just throws the dice and decides what it means."

As if to see how he might do such a thing, she examined the dice she held, two identical octahedrons and a cube. All three were black with white symbols. On seven faces the octahedrons reproduced the moon and star glyphs from the book; the eighth face on each was empty. The cube featured a face with a bar, another with a circle and four on which nothing showed.

Ekaterina was musing on her own comments and did not answer right away. Finally, she spoke.

"We all use it in different ways. We know it, individually, more or less well. Experience has shown that three types of people benefit from recourse to its wisdom."

She pointed vaguely off in an indication of her cousin.

"First are those who are highly intuitive. For them it provides a focus for clarifying the insights that come to them naturally." She waved her other hand to suggest a remove. "The second type are those who are not intuitive at all. It provides these with a framework for making decisions in circumstances where they do not have enough information. Generally with this sort you want to get a copy in their hands as early in life as possible."

She smiled at an unspoken thought and gave her head a wistful shake.

"You said three," Meg prompted. "That was only two."

"Oh, yes," Ekaterina picked up brightly. "And then there is everyone else, among whom I fall somewhere."

Meg tested the heft of the dice, rattled them a time or two, and tossed them onto the blanket alongside the swell of her leg.

"So Jack doesn't use the book because he doesn't know it very well?" she suggested tentatively.

"Dark of the moon and Daystar mean 'Repair.'" Ekaterina indicated the dice beside Meg. "Not a bad casual throw for an invalid. Quite the contrary, dear. Jackanapes does not use the book because he has it entire inside his head."

She gathered the dice and book, adroitly stowing all away, then again took up her spinning.

"He is, in fact, one of its great translators, having rendered it into both English and East Texican. As I said before, he really is quite a spectacular hybrid."

Something in this comment went through Meg like a shiver. Her gaze fell to the floor.

"Is he...the...is he the one...?" she trailed off.

"Would he father your child? No, not that one," answered the older woman. She relaxed, letting her spindle and fiber fall to her lap, and drew more intimately near as she spoke. "If you say yes, we shall ask you, when the time is right, to lie with one of Sweetheart's brothers. An energetic fellow we call Roamer."

"An elf?"

"A thrm, yes. You would truly find it most pleasant. Humans always find thrm'm to be the sweetest lovers. Sweet beyond imagination."

Meg blushed at this information but Ekaterina, almost blithely, did not notice.

"They are, after all, perfect empaths with an instinctual drive to nurture. That's why we ultimately had to remove them to residence in a non-contiguous consensus."

She clucked her tongue once and clasped her hands, palms up, one in the other. Looking off and up as she consulted the text of memory, her eyes narrowed as she spoke.

"When the Eurasian expansion was launched five and a half centuries ago it became clear that no place would be safe on this planet, particularly not for a species drawn to suffering with a compulsion to ease it. The Eurasian ideologies are founded upon the promulgation of suffering in order to maintain their ruling elites. Whenever the Eurasian ideologues have gotten their hands on a thrm...well, you can imagine. So we took them all away. All of them."

She threw up her hands and grinned at Meg. She was clearly pleased with what her people had chosen to do to protect the Thrm from humanity.

"We bring them back in small groups under our protection so they may conceive. We've removed most of our own populations also, particularly as you humans have come to foul more and more of the planet."

Jack suddenly burst back through the doorway.

"Hey, hey! Hello! I've got to say, Cousin, that I'm thinking it's time for a little something in the way of food. What do you think?"

Ekaterina snorted.

"I think you're suffering effects of testosterone intoxication," she replied.

"Mayhaps there, Cousin, but I'm famished all the same," he returned. "And I'll bet the darlings would care to dine if given the offer."

"Well, then," Ekaterina acquiesced, "This talkfest will just have to go on hold until the darlings and our dear boy have been fed."

"Hot dog!" Jack yelled. "Now we're talking! I'll pare and peel! I'll bake and boil! Just point me toward the makings!"

"A good thing you're most often too busy for sex when you're on assignment," his cousin observed dryly as she gathered her spinning materials into her bag. "Otherwise, given the appetite you get, the missions would be impossible to supply.

"Not to mention," she added, rising, "the amount of slang it seems to provoke in you. I mean, really, Jackanapes. Hot dog?"

# *Fifteen*

"YOU WANT ME TO HELP YOU take over the world," Meg accused.

"Not take it over, dear. We want you to help us save it."

Meg clung to her suspicions.

"How will making me have a baby help save the world? I don't get it."

Ekaterina had returned to Meg's side following the meal. Meg did not know what fare had been the thrm'ms' part, but for herself there had been a sweet and richly flavored soup spoon-fed to her by an amusingly attentive Jack. He had gone off again on his further adventures once all had been amply fed. The two woman now sat alone with each other.

"First of all, we cannot make you have the baby we hope you will choose to conceive. Such a thing is an absolute psycho-physiological impossibility. The Thrm may be ardent in pursuit of the procreative act, but the most fundamental fact of their being is that they are empaths. They exist as individuals within an externally determined group emotional state."

Ekaterina's hands flew at her spinning, her rocking a governing rhythm to the forming thread.

"They are incapable of arousal when confronted with a non-reciprocating partner. The egoistic volition necessary to press their will is foreign to them. On the other hand, as externally determined empaths, you can imagine the satisfactions they might provide to a willing lover. Before we withdrew them from this consensus there were numerous cases of the poor dears dying as sex slaves of libidinous humans."

Meg began defensively, "You know, I don't think I understand everything you're saying—"

Ekaterina cut her off. "Oh, but I think you do." Her eyes fairly glittered now. "But let me address this for you in the most transparent terms. Listen carefully."

Meg was surprised at the pique of shame she felt for provoking Ekaterina's anger. She had still half believed that she was looking for a way to resist what she assumed were captors—albeit of an unusual sort—while it seemed that she was actually beginning to hear this strange, nut brown woman as an ally. She could see that her pretense of not understanding had offended Ekaterina in a personal way. For reasons Meg had to admit she understood, the dvarsh had taken a smart person playing dumb as an insult. The sudden, vigorous rocking that accompanied the elder woman's change of tone suggested a kind of agitation better left to run its course than interdicted, even for an apology.

Ekaterina had stopped spinning when she had interrupted Meg. She now continued, measuring her words by the lengths of twisted fiber taken up on her spindle.

"First, life on this world—in this consensus—is direly threatened. The agent of catastrophe is human, so called civilization," the dvarsh spoke this last word as though it tasted bad when she said it, "which has been wreaking havoc with the planet—meaning living systems on the planet, meaning life on the planet, meaning the living planet—for these last not too few millennia."

She sighed, slowed, took on a wistful note.

"All along it could have been better—better, cleaner, fairer choices were available—and in some places they took them. For a while, for a time. The loving way always takes a little more effort, a little more thought. Because of that, more quiet, more pause. So easily obstructed. So easily overrun. And then forever we spend searching for our shattered clans, our lost tribes."

Ekaterina's attention had drifted away from Meg to someplace on a distant, unapparent horizon. She came back to the room with a sharp breath and a slap of her thigh.

"Be that as it may, in the last five hundred years the destruction has escalated, most particularly in the last two hundred. The population of humans has burgeoned until it shrouds the landmasses, forming huge patches of high density that produce noise and glare and accumulations of toxins, septic filth. It is all so completely frivolous."

She began again to rock faster and faster as she spoke.

"Think about it and the stupidities multiply: Wage slavery, male supremacy, nation states, the petroleum industry, it goes on and on. Patrilineage. Land hunger. Race myths. You just cannot really know how disturbing it is to have to watch such huge masses of people—humans, yes, but clearly people all the same—living with such transparently self-defeating values. Like body taboos, or a popular music 'industry,' or institutional religion. Rupturing atoms. Private cars. Powerlust. Property rights. Mineral rights. Water rights. Rights of way. Pah! Rights, rights, rights! It is our home, too!"

At this point Ekaterina was so agitated that she broke off and began to spin furiously, all the while taking deep, regular breaths. Meg looked on as the dvarsh woman absorbed the agitation back into herself, reshaped it, made it a steadiness. She waited for Ekaterina again to speak. After several minutes, she did speak, her voice low and calm. She continued spinning.

"For us, the first lesson we are taught is the interconnection, the allness of each thing, the world's tremendous sensitivity. The bad effects are cumulative. The stresses take their toll. It is like after a hard winter, when the food has been scarce, the spring fawns are smaller and weaker, taking ill more easily. And they, in turn, produce fawns weak and sickly. Only you must multiply that by all the people and all the minutes and all the stupidities to calculate the effect."

Ekaterina paused in her spinning.

"Do you know what a hellhound is?" she asked, locking her eyes to Meg's.

The young woman was startled by the sudden intensity of Ekaterina's focus.

"Excuse me?" she said.

"A hellhound," her companion repeated. "I shall tell you, child. A hellhound is a greasy, dirty, smelly rack of bones." She stopped rocking and spinning, and waved her spindle like a baton counting time to her words. "It is greasy and dirty because it lives in an environment contaminated by filth and waste on every side, and it cannot get clean. It is starving because it has little to eat and what it has is unwholesome. It breathes with a wheeze because of constant exposure to noxious vapors, and it has open sores from the agents that have leached into the ground where it is condemned to seek its rest. But its rest has been banished and it has been driven insane by the constant noise to which it is subjected. It is so hungry that in desperation it will attack anything, no matter how it is outmatched. Its desperation will drive it to break itself in a thousand ways, while preventing it from ever giving up. A hellhound will dig through rock trying to make a meal of a mouse, a mite. It may be sick, but it is still implacable, unstoppable. And it has nowhere to go."

She allowed her spindle to fall to her lap.

"I'm afraid something like that is in store for us."

"Excuse me?" Meg said again, surprised back from concentrating on the picture of such a desperate beast.

"Oh, yes. We know this is happening. There are already pockets where the decline is obvious. Urbania for the most part. The struggle for redirection is almost ten thousand years old, intense for five hundred. The Long War, we call it. The current intensification that has sickened you is but one more phase. Our struggle is unremitting, unrelenting, continuous. If we lose this consensus, we lose all. It is only here that we can conceive."

Ekaterina paused. She stretched, arching her back, and raising her hands, spindle and all, above her head before allowing them to sink again to her lap.

"But there are many reasons to hope. Most of our work is quiet and behind the scenes. We teach life without so many chemicals, the practice of uncrowding, a lessening of noise, and less owning. Much less owning. We seek the bold and tender among humans who might assist us in turning the stampede, who will let us infiltrate with our genes, both thrm and dvarsh."

Meg could sense that Ekaterina was winding down. The intensity of her delivery was less and she still sat without rocking. Meg felt that it might be the moment for her to raise the question that most concerned her.

"How could I have this baby you want?" she asked, then hurried on, "It's bad enough for me, growing up with no mother and having to work and not having very much money. You know how people are. You know what kinds of things they say. You know how they treat girls who have babies when they don't have husbands. How could I go through that?"

"Primitives, yes. Your people are such ridiculous primitives, thinking all their machines and roads and cities and little sciences make them better than they are." Ekaterina pursed her lips and blew through them noisily. "Among the truly civilized, among the Dvarsh for instance, who the father of a child may be is considered the business of no one but the mother. No one. It would be rude for even close kin to ask. The mother alone tracks the genetics."

Meg looked at her incredulously.

"I am serious, dear," the older woman insisted. "In a true civilization marriage is rare. A bond chosen only by those special couples who seek a different order of spiritual life by reserving themselves for each other."

"But, Ekaterina. I'm a human. Humans aren't like that. Not here. Not in this country."

"Of that," Ekaterina responded, "I am too well aware. But even so, even here, that is going to improve. At least somewhat. At least enough. And sooner than you think, Meg. I give you my word that it will change enough to make you safe. At least for the term that you will need."

"But if I have this baby, what will it mean? I'm just eighteen years old. And my father's dead. I'm going to go to college—I have a scholarship. How would I support it? I don't really have anything. What will happen to me?"

This last came out as nearly a wail.

"Poor child. Of course, you're frightened. I promise you, in all the difficult times we shall be with you to help. But that won't be for a long time. I forgot you would assume that this would be an ordinary human pregnancy. Truth is, when a thrm man inseminates a human woman his sperm remains in her womb for at least eight and perhaps as long as fifteen years before it fertilizes an egg. It is a result of the different hormonal environment humans provide." Ekaterina was again explaining in her unselfconsciously professorial manner. "No one really knows why. It's generally agreed that the effect is due to differences in human and thrm'mic biochemistry. In any case, it averages a dozen years before conception follows consummation, possibly even longer in the case of certain metabolic conditions. Am I embarrassing you?"

Meg had reddened, but shook her head no.

"Good. Even when thrm mates with thrm it takes about two years between insemination and fertilization. With a human woman, as I said, it takes much, much longer. So you see it could be anywhere from your calendar's mid-century to, say, the middle of its seventh decade before you were pregnant in any sense that you understand. In the meantime, the presence of the thrm'mic sperm would act as an absolutely safe, absolutely effective contraceptive—which you might find pleasant. You would, of course, require normal, responsible precautions against disease.

"But the big difficulty facing you if you agree is that we would need to keep you here, in this cabin, in these mountains, over the winter."

"Keep me?" Meg was clearly thrown by the suggestion. Her voice was nearly a whisper. "Keep me here?"

"Yes, Meg. Even so, it will be a short term for the amount of instruction we have to cover."

"But I have plans. I'm going to college. I have a scholarship."

"College will be waiting for you when you come down. You will see."

Meg averted her eyes and chewed her lip for a moment.

"Ekaterina?"

"Yes, child?"

"Would my baby be like Jesus?"

Ekaterina erupted in roaring laughter.

"Jackanapes, that rascal. He did fill your head with stuff. I'm afraid we can't make any promises about the child. It could be a great teacher or healer, or it could not. Often the mix produces beach bums, palm readers, jazz musicians, circus folk—people whose dissent from the mainstream the human elite consider marginal, irrelevant. One never knows. That boy Yeshua was one of ours, yes, and it is possible there could be another like him—but such a pack of lies they tell now about poor Miriam's son. Of course, even that situation is better than another one like Rataxes. An unlikely possibility with you but less so with some others."

"That general is a hybrid?" Meg gasped.

"Third generation re-bred human from a full mix," Ekaterina answered. "We're still trying to determine where we went wrong. But he is, after all, the only one like him we've ever seen."

"Seems like he's taken care of furnishing more examples all on his own."

Meg could not help smirking as she said this.

"Well, yes. But Rataxes apart, the point is the genes themselves and their future generations. We don't know what kind of person your baby would turn out to be. There are limits to the amount of certainty about a given future one can pull from even the most strenuous application of the disciplines. We do, however, think your child would be a boy."

"Why do you say that?"

"Patience, Meg. You can't have all of Being unveiled at a single sitting. It would give you a terrible case of runny bowels. For now, let's stay with my question."

"Your question?"

"The only question at the moment. Will you do it?"

Meg gripped the blanket tightly with both hands. She let her eyes unfocus as her mouth went dry. The pounding of her heart became an ache in her chest. The moment hung, waiting for her next words. At last she turned again to the other woman and spoke.

"Ekaterina, I...I don't know. I don't think I can."

Ekaterina sagged in her chair. Before Meg's eyes she suddenly looked old and tired. Her voice quavered slightly as she replied.

"Well, never mind. We still have to finish making you well. I shall get Sweetheart to feed you, and then you must sleep."

# *Sixteen*

A FEW DAYS AFTER DECLINING TO breed Ekaterina's wished-for babe, Meg woke for the second time in a morning, on this occasion to find the older woman beside her cot, offering a cup of steaming, aromatic beverage. Her first waking had been a bare bump into consciousness when Sweetheart lifted Meg's head to nurse. Gray had just outlined the window's shutters through the darkness. At that instance, Meg roused only enough to help the thrm woman's effort actually bring lips to tit; this second time, however, the cabin felt entirely, unexpectedly empty of thrm'm. Unanticipated silence brought Meg more sharply awake.

"Meg, dear, while it's hot I'd like you to drink this."

Ekaterina held the heavy white ceramic cup away from her body as she slipped her free arm behind Meg to raise her unjarred to a sitting position. Meg took the cup from Ekaterina, but held it without tasting as her head cleared from the strain of sitting up.

"It smells...good," she said finally, a note of surprise in her voice. "What's in it?"

"Oh, good things, wonderful things. Cinnamon and licorice root and a little ginger, just a tiny bit of cayenne pepper..."

"Pepper!"

Meg stared at the cup with sudden suspicion.

"Please, dear, try it before you make up your mind."

Meg sipped.

"It's kind of thick," she said.

"That's the slippery elm," Ekaterina responded. "The main point, really. The other things mostly add savor."

"It's kind of strange. But it's good. I think."

She sipped again.

"It's really good. What else is in it?"

"Good things. Special things. Things to make you healthy. Flowers. Spice."

Meg held the mug close to her face, both hands clasped around it, enjoying its warmth. Occasionally, she would sip. Her mind seemed elsewhere.

Abruptly, she looked at Ekaterina and asked, "Where are the thrm'm?"

"Outside," the dvarsh answered. "Playing in the sun. It's a beautiful day."

The words tugged at Meg, causing her to start.

"Could I go outside?" she asked.

Ekaterina first looked at her doubtfully.

"Child, you are still recovering from the last time you got up."

"Ekaterina, I don't want to run away. I just want to get off this cot for a while." She willed herself to project hopeful sufficiency. "I'd like to sit in the sun. Please?"

The older woman's expression softened.

"I suppose some time in the sun would work to your benefit."

So saying, she sat erect, clapped her hands and called, "Jackanapes! Up, lingerer. We require assistance!"

Jack sat up immediately beside the cot on the side away from his cousin. He turned his face this way and that, blinking rapidly and smacking his lips like he had a bad taste in his mouth.

"Rise, dear boy. Your hand is needed."

He scrambled from the floor and jerked to attention.

"Jack Plenty up and ready for using, Cousin." He swooped his head back and forth in a dramatic examination of things right and left. "What's the work?"

"Jackanapes, I want you to turn your back to us and hold your arms behind you. I am going to help Meg out of the bed. I want you, without looking, to hold her up while I dress her. "

He scowled.

"Not even one look?"

"None," Ekaterina admonished.

He turned to Meg.

"You don't mind if old Jack takes an eyeful, do you?"

"Ekaterina!" Meg objected sharply.

"Jackanapes, she says 'no' and that closes the issue. But quite apart from that, she's been gravely ill. Why would you relish the sight of a still recovering body?"

"But that's the point, Cousin. Poetical research. You know, all forms the organism takes, that sort of thing. For the benefit of my work."

"Another time, I think, dear boy. Just now we need your back turned, your arms behind you and your eyes forward. Please."

Jack bobbed his head and mugged, but did as requested.

Ekaterina helped Meg to swing her legs over the side of the cot. Then she slid herself under one of the younger woman's arms, putting her own limb around Meg's waist. With a quick brace of one foot and spin on the ball of the other she whirled Meg off the cot, up and against Jack's back in a single circular motion. Jack laced his fingers behind his back, drawing his broad shoulders up and to the rear, setting his elbows akimbo Ekaterina draped Meg's arms over his shoulders as over a rack. Meg slipped her arms back through Jack's and gripped his forearms to keep from sliding to the floor. The difference in their heights would have been too great except he leaned forward slightly so her weight rested a little above his rump. Meg was sure the posture and her bulk must be uncomfortable for him, but Jack stood uncomplaining.

"You're still a touch on the warm side," he told her. "Sure you want to do this?"

"Yes," Meg answered in a voice soft but firm.

Ekaterina, in the meantime, had produced not a set of Meg's familiar clothes, but a duplicate of the thick garments that swathed her own body. Over and around Meg she draped and wrapped and tucked and looped soft, dvarsh-woven fabric. Meg was astonished at the feel of the clothing. They seemed secure on her, but at the same time loose fitting and unrestrictive. She was thoroughly covered, even to a shawl-like fold over her head, but felt unconfined. The garments enveloped her, comforted her, seemed to provide her with a measure of the stability fever had shaken, but without making her feel burdened in any way. More than just the joy of being once more out of bed and clad in a dignified fashion, she was touched by the pleasure of wearing these articles of dress.

"I love these clothes," she told the woman who swathed her.

"They are no more than our own homespun," observed Ekaterina. "The same fiber your mothers spun for generations, but spun by us as prayer, and woven, too, by our own methods."

"Spun as prayer?" Meg repeated. "Is that what your spinning is? What you do? What Jack does?"

"It is for us like what prayer should be for you. It is not asking for anything. It is taking a sacred gift and using it for making, a making as a symbol of the way the world is daily made, and doing so without despoliation. A clean making that gives back the same measure it takes. For each of us, to spin is to lose oneself in the doing, and to do in such a way that our body remembers the interconnection. "

They had moved through the cabin as Ekaterina spoke, Meg leaning heavily on both of her companions. Stepping to the open doorway, Meg saw the Thrm, dozens cavorting, rolling on the meadow grasses, lying staring at the sky, propped on elbows staring at the ground, leapfrogging, mating, chasing insects or plant stuff that floated on the wind, singing, singing, all of them singing, each an individual song like a horde of canaries talking to themselves, but the impression of the whole was of a single web or lattice of music.

The next instant they were every one silent and motionless, upright and staring toward some far point in the forest. In the cessation of their voices, Meg heard faintly a shrill repeating cry, or thought she heard it. If it was sound it was so faint she was not sure she heard something separate from the whistling in the wind. She wasn't sure it was sound, thinking maybe it was something different but that sound was the only way she had of understanding it.

Jack sprang away from her, bellowing, "Little buddy!"

His fiber stock and raw thread rained behind him as he threw things from his bag while galloping toward the forest's edge, neighing like an angry stallion. The thrm'm, as one, gripped their sticks, raised them over their heads and raced off the same way.

"Wolves!" Ekaterina cried, as Meg heard now sounds of the pack. "They've cornered Roamer."

She pulled Meg back into the cabin and sat her on a chair.

"Stay put. Jackanapes will pound the poor things if I don't get there first. His bag is always heavy with stones."

With this, she ran from the cabin, twirled once, her cloak billowing so that it, first, hid her, and then settled itself into nothingness.

Meg stared for a moment at the place the other woman had last occupied, but then let her eyes go out of focus. It was odd that Ekaterina's disappearance had not disturbed her, but she had to admit it had not. She was fairly certain she could stand, walk to the door, close it and return to her chair without falling, if she so chose, but she affirmed this to herself more as a reassurance than a preliminary to action.

Motionless, she sat as the sun crept slowly through the door, over her toes, then up her foot toward her ankle. She was aware of the warmth on that foot, liked it, relished it, but made no move to place herself more fully in the light. Through the stillness that had dropped like a curtain, a jay swooped, landing, she thought, on or near the tower. It barked twice in a raspy voice, then gave a shrill, piercing whistle. Meg thought it must be one that she had fed several times over the summer. A woodpecker's exploratory raps came from some point on the meadow's lower edge.

Thoughts stopped dead, she sat with eyes fixed to the infinite. Sounds reached her from outside the cabin, none loud, none close, but she had ceased identifying them. The collective sensations of her body, the post fever ache in her joints, the sun warmed foot, the light drag of her unfamiliar garments against her skin were experienced intensely but namelessly. She was aware of a speech-like buzzing in her head, the commentator remote somewhere behind her outlook, persistent still but fading as from accelerating distance, already beyond any threshold of comprehensibility.

She saw the eyes first in her mind before she realized that she was seeing them through the open door of the cabin. She refocused. A lone wolf, a large male, gray with black points, stood a few feet outside the doorway, staring at her. Other than her eyes she remained motionless, but the wolf, when their gazes met, took a step forward and stretched his muzzle in her direction. He sniffed loudly several times, recoiled a half step, then brushed his nose with his foreleg like he had stuck it into something unpleasant. He met her eyes again, holding the contact while he seemed to contemplate the situation.

After looking once over his shoulder in the direction taken by Jack and the thrm'm, the wolf walked to the doorway, lifted his leg and urinated onto the frame. Finished, he scratched stiffly and fiercely at the ground with his hind feet. Satisfied with this display he stood at right angles to the door, looking expectantly back toward the edge of the meadow.

Almost immediately, Jack, Ekaterina and the thrm'm stepped out of the forest. Roamer, apparently unharmed, showed a broadly berry stained face from his perch on Jack's shoulders. Jack, in turn, was interrupting a lecture by Ekaterina.

"But, Jackanapes," she was saying, "If you hurt any of them it could void the understanding..."

"We're talking my little buddy here, Cousin," Jack insisted.

"It is our responsibility to keep them safe, not the wolves' to avoid eating them," she countered. Then she saw the wolf at the door.

"Oh, dear Gussie, no! Meg!" she cried as once again she twirled and her cloak billowed out, then settled into nothingness.

The wolf, having been seen, trotted insouciantly away. Ekaterina reached from behind Meg, embracing her.

"Dear child, are you all right?"

"Yes," Meg answered. "I'm fine."

She settled back into the older woman's arms and allowed her head to loll back onto the other's shoulder.

"Why do you think he wanted to see me?" she asked.

"Of course," Ekaterina exclaimed. "That must be it. That gray dog staged this in order to get a look at you."

# Seventeen

"THEY'RE INTENSELY CURIOUS ABOUT ANY INTERACTIONS we have with humans, the wolves are. I think they may be wondering whether limited contact might benefit them and they are trying to gauge our experience."

Ekaterina talked as she lit the stove and filled the kettle.

"They eat the darlings!" Jack roared, having heard the last statement as he approached the door. The thrm on his shoulders was warbling effusively and, as effusively, patting, massaging and hugging Jack's head.

"They're carnivorous empaths," Ekaterina snapped. "They are perfectly adapted for preying upon other empathic species. But they and we have an understanding, dvarsh and wolf, and not you, not anyone else can jeopardize that."

"I'm not all dvarsh, you know," he shot back. "The little ones are also what I am. I've got more than one line to stand in, as the facts would have it."

Jack dropped heavily into one of the ladderback chairs at the table where Meg was seated, keeping Roamer astride his neck as he did so. The thrm bubbled happily, patting Jack's head or waving his hands gracefully as he sang to the room.

Ekaterina softened some.

"Indeed you do. But the point remains that they smell you as dvarsh and it is with the dvarsh alone that they have arrived at an understanding."

"What sort of understanding can you have with wolves?" Meg interjected.

She had remained passively seated to this point. Now she stirred as she posed her question.

Ekaterina set out four of the white ceramic mugs. From her bag she took a teaball and a small tin, filling the teaball with an herbal mix from the tin. Removing the now boiling kettle from the heat, she dropped the tea ball directly into it. With a spoon she pushed the tea ball around in the kettle until satisfied with the color, then filled the four cups. Reaching again into her bag she produced a small, shallow, wide-mouthed container of brown glass capped with a garishly decorated enameled metal lid. This held a light colored paste from which Ekaterina scraped only a tiny fraction. This she stirred into one of the mugs and a smell of flowers filled the room.

She lifted the thrm from her cousin's shoulders, placing him on another chair at the table. Dipping her fingers into the strongly scented cup, she raised them to Roamer's lips for tasting. He responded with a chuttered sigh of approval and reached for the beverage. Ekaterina stopped him. She held his hand close to the mug so he could feel the heat. Then she lifted another cup, blew across the tea, took a tiny sip, blew across the tea, took a tiny sip, then motioned to Roamer to copy her. This the little man did, and was soon immersed in the alternation of sipping and blowing. Ekaterina gave Jack and Meg each a cup. Meg was about to restate her question when the older woman finally spoke.

"Dvarsh harm no wolves; wolves harm no dvarsh. It's a recognition that when we war neither of us escapes grievous wounding. It's a recognition, though—an understanding. Not a thing that has been negotiated. We could not, say, add terms to include the Thrm. Actually, Jackanapes has composed a poem about it."

"You really like his poetry?"

Meg winced with incredulity.

"Child, Jackanapes is one of our greatest poets."

"That's right. One of the greatest," Jack agreed.

"But do you think they're any good? Jack's poems, I mean."

"Oh, I'm sure they are. Absolutely. He works very hard at them, positively perseverant in fine tuning distinctions that are no more than incalculable increments to me. Certainly they are good. I enjoy his recitations immensely. Like the poem of the understanding with the wolves. Jackanapes." She turned to her cousin. "Speak it for us. Let Meg hear how finely you compose."

Never one needing to be asked twice, Jack stood and assumed his performance posture—shoulders squared, head up, feet apart, one hand on his breast, the other hand clenched loosely at the small of his back—and offered his title:

*"At the Tree Where We Pee with the Wolves"*

He adjusted his stance, cleared his throat, wiggled his eyebrows once at Meg, and began to recite:

> *"In the woods the doggie's dance, their coats erect,*
> *their hackles up like a jillion quivering antennae*
> *receiving on the shortened frequencies, plugged direct,*
> *mouths agape and tongues nimble in the rapid shrug*
> *of a thousand pants, the dance of the wooddog,*
> *the rangy wolf, all toothy mouthed and so correct,*
> *lovey dear to her pups, little fuzzy spud pups*
> *too stupid to do anything but tug*
> *at your biddy heartstrings. Same dancing dog,*
> *all toothy, that wolf sees a little buddy, eats him!*
> *That wolfie thinks come-on-down-here thoughts*
> *like a backless sheath, a slinky, strapless velvet thing*
> *on Myrna Loy, make that Marlene Dietrich, no,*
> >  *Gene Tierney,*
> *ah, Gene Tierney, or some smart beauty all razor wit*
> *and soft come hither, call you, 'Hey there, boy,'*
> *back from your box at the wake to trade*
> *the stone person that sits in your middle, the grade*
> *of your soul, that wolfie, that dancing wooddog*
> *sees a buddy, wants him, wants him! Little buddy*
> *wants to live, but lives to please, to please, to please*
> *and feels the way wolfie looks at him and sees*
> *a tasty dinner! Little buddy freezes…"*

"You seem to have added some new material at the beginning, Jackanapes," Ekaterina interrupted. "I did not remember so much on the wolf's manner of hunting thrm'm. I had thought it proceeded more directly to the understanding between wolves and dvarsh."

"I was coming to it," Jack said, dropping leadenly back into his seat. "You know, Cousin, you really can't hurry an artist in the throes of wrestling with, um, you know, the muse."

Roamer leaned over to pat Jack's leg and chuttered consolingly, though he kept his other hand tightly around his mug.

"Is that what you were doing?"

She looked him directly in the eye as she asked.

"Well, yeah. Some," Jack replied, suddenly sullen. "I was feeling some juice there for a minute."

At that instant a thrm, throwing its stick to one side as it entered, bounded through the door, up to Jack and began with all six fingers and four thumbs to press and rub around the base of his skull. Almost immediately, Jack relaxed, leaning back into the massage. Warbling sweetly, Roamer reached up his free hand to dance his fingers over Jack's face.

"Cousin, let's get back to more of that poetry later, what do you say?" he proposed, his eyes closed, his arms going limp.

"As you wish, dear boy," she agreed, producing her spindle. "My own composure would benefit if I gave the next hour or so to spinning."

The thrm working on the base of Jack's skull leaned around to catch her eye and sang a questioning line.

"No, don't draw anyone in for me, dear. I need to do this for myself. Another time."

With that, the dvarsh drew her spinning from her bag, efficiently arranging the turns of fiber and the disposition of her implements.

Meg watched with fixed attention as the fiber transformed through Ekaterina's fingers. She followed the spindle drop, and the quick whip as the older woman took up the thread. Meg watched in silence. She knew that if she spoke, if she questioned Ekaterina, the other would respond, but she had learned that her dvarsh friend preferred to spin without distraction, movements quickly becoming regularized, eyes looking into other possible realities, accompanying herself with an almost inaudible humming as she spun thread to make herself one with the making of the world.

# Eighteen

"So. How do you travel?" Meg asked.

It was the day after Meg and Roamer had had their respective encounters with wolves. The two women were talking in Meg's room, Ekaterina in her rocker and Meg on her cot, propped by pillows.

"How do we travel? Why, we walk, we ride trains—"

"No," Meg cut her off. "I mean how do you travel between where you live and here?"

"From consensus to consensus?" Ekaterina's head dropped and craned forward as she gazed at Meg with an expression of anticipation. A suggestion of a smile played about her mouth.

"Right. From consensus to consensus." Meg twice pronounced the unfamiliar term carefully. "How do you, you know, get to the one you want if there are so many?"

"Well," Ekaterina's cheeks dimpled as she began to explain, "frankly, the process relies ultimately on an element of faith. Not a large element, but significant nonetheless. There is a great deal of discipline to it, and for those like me that is the most important thing. Jackanapes, however, is another matter. Discipline of any sort is beyond him, so his reliance is on his extraordinary intuition. Not that it doesn't steer him wrong occasionally, at least when he solos. You wouldn't believe some of the scrapes we've pulled him from when he's dropped into the wrong consensus at the wrong time. Once he even caused our whole team to drop a degree off mark when he failed to sufficiently clear his mind of libidinous influences. We manifested in the middle of a Roman orgy. At least that's what it seemed until we got our bearings. Actually, it turned out to be a holiday observance by a student society on a university campus in a parallel consensus. I must say, they could have had better sex with less alcohol and more solicitude toward their partners. We continue to hope that this sort of thing might be less of a problem as Jackanapes matures through the next half century. This past half has presented challenges."

Ekaterina paused here and drew a snuff box from within a fold of her clothing. She inhaled a pinch into each nostril, sneezed three times, rapidly, then replaced the snuffbox and went on, turning back from reminiscence to Meg's query.

"Any one of us in the struggle can jump alone. Jumping is one of the things that defines the thoroughness of our education. If one can't jump, then one has only been indoctrinated, not educated in the reason, means and necessity of the struggle. That's true no matter how easily one may field questions from an examiner. But solo jumping is most often limited to emergencies and a kind of final exam we undertake before being loosed as free agents in the struggle for life. The fact I've been doing so much of it alone recently is a sign of how dire we find the times. Most often we jump in teams we call Threes Out Of Four."

"I heard Jack use that term," Meg said.

Ekaterina nodded and continued, "Jackanapes and I are working as a binary unit right now because my sister, Mathilde, our 'pataphysician, has soloed into central Europe to work as a disruptive influence. Each Three Out Of Four has a 'pataphysician, a metamathemage and an intuit. I am an Exemplary Metamathemage, of the thirty-three and a third order of magnitude, and Mathilde (whom I hope you one day meet) is a thirty-fourth dimensional Grand Rapscalliar 'Pataphysician with gold reputational clusters. Jackanapes, the dear boy, as you've probably guessed, is our intuit. His theory's a garble, but he's vital, quite vital, all the same."

Ekaterina was positively beaming at Meg as she paused again for another pinch of snuff. Her pleasure in the subject was transparent. The younger woman, however, was distracted by her friend's powder.

"Why do you use that stuff?" Meg asked her. "My grandmother used to say tobacco is the devil's weed."

"And so it is," Ekaterina returned, "in the hands of those who profane it. A most holy herb in the hands of those who respect and fear it. But this mix is not tobacco. Rather, a blend of powdered burdock and licorice root, with a healthy dose of cinnamon and a dash of damiana. My method of administration is peculiar, but the dvarsh of my clan have preferred to take it so. We clear our lungs by leaving the residue when we jump."

Meg's brow furrowed as she digested this.

"Is that a regular part of how you jump?"

Ekaterina chuckled.

"No, just one of my clan's shortcuts to health. How we jump, or pull, or push, involves specific mind links among the three. Pulling or pushing are ways that we move objects or others between consensa."

"Like thrm'm?"

"No," the elder smiled. "The Thrm we handle a different way. We pull or push humans or our own tyros or gear or whatnot. Pulling and pushing involve the same kinds of responsibilities as jumping. With the aid of the intuit, the 'pataphysician and metamathemage link and begin to simultaneously perform specialized and highly focused lucubrations. After a crucial vectoring, it's whip, skip, and bing! You're there. No unwieldy transports necessary."

The broad, brown dvarsh evidenced a personal satisfaction with her culture's accomplishments. She seemed to radiate pride as she spoke.

"But how do you bring the elves?" Meg asked.

"The Thrm? They are empaths. When we have linked we draw on their empathy to get them to attach to us."

"How do you get them to want to?"

"That is the easiest and the hardest thing in the world. The how of it is almost impossible to explain, but once the knack is learned it is never lost. The trick is in what's most attractive to an empath, at least one whose instinct is to nurture. They do make choices, you must have observed. The people they most often choose to approach are those for whom the pleasure of the Thrm is their own pleasure. So, when we want them to attach, we love them."

"You love them? That's all?"

"All? There's no all to it." Ekaterina laughed. "We have to radiate to them with a deliberate and uncritically active love. The thing is, you can never know how many will attach to the process. Usually all who are in range of the ray of affection. It gets complicated."

Meg mulled this explanation for a moment. When she spoke again she had set it aside and returned to earlier words.

"If you're thirty-three and a third magnitude and your sister is thirty-fourth, what magnitude is Jack."

"Actually," Ekaterina said confidingly, "I am thirty-three and a third magnitude—thirty-two plus one to grow on, and a little bit for lagniappe—but Mathilde is thirty-fourth dimensional. My cousin, on the other hand, is an intuit and that is a different case altogether. They have neither degree nor rank. One either is or is not sufficiently intuitive. There are greater and lesser ranges of intuition, but the Guild of Intuits recognizes no distinctions among any sufficiently intuitive to complete the initiation. If you are one of them you are one of them and that is all there is to the matter. Jackanapes is absolutely remarkable in his degree of intuition, but his lack of discipline is not uncharacteristic of the guild as a whole."

Ekaterina arched her back and stretched her arms over her head. She dropped them quickly to use one hand stifling a yawn.

"I'm afraid you've quite worn me out with your asking, dear. We should begin thinking about another tonifying decoction. Followed by rest."

She began to rise.

"Before we stop, may I ask another question? Well, two questions, really."

The dvarsh sank back into her chair.

"Yes, child. Please. Ask."

"What are 'pataphysics and metamathemagic?"

"Metamathemagics," Ekaterina stressed the terminal 's.' "They are the higher sciences of true understanding. 'Pataphysics deals exclusively with the particular, including, of course, the ramifications and tactics of particularity, which is to say, all things that are exceptional. Metamathemagics, my discipline," she seemed to glow as she spoke, even to inflate a little, "involves the observation and manipulation of the unquantifiable aspects of quantifiable phenomena. If you will think of the Three Out Of Four as a vehicle, the metamathemage pilots, the 'pataphysician navigates and the intuit provides the propulsive force. At this point, if I tried to be more explicit than that I'm afraid you would be completely lost."

"I am completely lost," Meg confirmed. "Sort of. I think."

"It will all seem much clearer after you have eaten something—real food today, not just thrm's milk and broth. That, and some time to sleep will make all things clearer."

"I think even after I sleep I won't understand why you're a 'Three out of Four.' If you're three out of four, whose the fourth? And if, like Jackanapes says, three out of four isn't bad does that mean the fourth one would be wicked?"

Ekaterina smiled at her.

"Hardly ever wicked. The fourth we always find when we get where we're going."

Meg's heartbeat quickened as the implications of this statement sank in.

"So, you're saying I'm the fourth in your group right now?"

"Exactly so. At this time, at this place, in this consensus."

This thought pleased Meg to a degree that surprised her. She liked feeling like one of them, a part of their struggle. At that moment she was feeling tired, worn out from her long conversation. She settled down into her covers as Ekaterina once more raised herself from the chair and started toward the door. Meg thought to doze while her meal was prepared, hoping to find strength to continue talking later. Just before the other left the room Meg spoke again.

"Does the word 'ick-and-ee' mean something?"

Ekaterina spun toward her, blinking with astonishment.

"What did you say?" she demanded. "What was that?"

"Ick-and-ee. At least, I think that's how you would say it."

"What are you trying to say? What word? Spell it."

"I-c-a-n-d-y."

"Icandy! Icandy!" The older woman pronounced the word 'eye candy,' "How do you know anything about that? Where did you learn of this?"

"I saw it." Meg faltered. "I mean, I guess I saw it. It was one of the times Sweetheart was patting on my face. My thoughts got slow and went away. This moving pattern filled up the place in my mind where my thinking usually is. Then I saw that word floating in front of the pattern." She waved her hand weakly as if to denote her mental space. "What does it mean?"

Ekaterina had reached out her hand and was leaning on the doorframe, struggling to recover from bafflement.

"Remarkable," she spoke as to herself. "Remarkable," she repeated. "Yes, it does mean something, although it's not a word really. It's more of a formula, I would say. Specifically, it's the metamathemagical expression of the cross-consensual jump."

"You're kidding."

It was Meg's turn to register surprise.

"No, dear, I am not." Ekaterina stood free of the doorframe, her habitual calm returned. "The pattern you refer to could only be the directed visualizations that represent the metamathemagical lucubrations of the jumplink among the three. This is truly astonishing. This was a passive experience for you?"

"I...yes. I mean, I just watched it happen. I didn't do anything to make it change or go on or anything. Is something wrong?"

"Wrong? No, dear. But this is going to call for some directed thinking. I'm aware of no case in the literature that resembles it."

"What does it mean?"

"That, my child, we can only tell by waiting to see."

# Nineteen

MEG AND EKATERINA SAT TOGETHER BESIDE Mr. Christmas's grave. Except for assisted trips to the outhouse, it was Meg's first day out of the cabin since the aborted attempt on the day of the wolf's visit. Like Ekaterina she was protected from the autumn chill by fat layers of dvarsh cloaks and wraps. Her human sweaters and coat remained stowed in their old wooden chest.

Jack tried to sit with them, but kept leaping up and racing back to the cabin, charging inside to join the copulating frolic of the thrm'm. Few of the small folk had even made it out the door that morning. After an absence of half an hour or so, he would return to fidget beside the two women, chiming in now and again with a not always relevant comment. They sat on large, squat sections of log, nearly as wide as tall. Mr. Christmas, by dent of strenuous labor, had once placed these in front of the cabin, and there would perch to survey the grand vista that opened out in the space beyond their clearing in the trees.

The grave was placed at the high end of the clearing, at a level higher than the cabin roof but not so high as the observation deck of the watch tower. The space between cabin and grave amounted more to a small meadow than to a mere yard, and was matched by about as much space again down slope in front of the structures. At its widest the clearing was slightly less than half the measure of its total length. Although they could not see it, Meg knew the tree line sat above them about three times the open area's length. She knew also that just within the forest edge the slope behind them rose much more sharply.

Plucking a grass stalk that had dropped its seeds, Meg wondered who had moved their seats uphill from the cabin. Dense, still resinous wood, each one weighed more than she did by a good measure. To roll the lengths of bole a nearly level course—from where she had helped him saw down a lightning-struck tree all the way to the sheltered area in front of the cabin—had taken her father a great deal of huffing and puffing and several pauses for colorful language. Vividly, she recalled the two of them sectioning out these impulsive pieces of furniture, her father wrestling them close to the house while she was left to split the rest. Intrigued by the question of how the great logs had reached their present location, she studied the slope below her for indications of scuffing or gouging that might have occurred during a strenuous uphill roll. As she did so, Jack bounded back from one of his visits to the cabin. A shadow had moved across his previous seat during his absence. The high, early autumn air was too chill to bear without sun and Meg expected him to move to the far side of Ekaterina, where a fourth section still sat squarely in the afternoon rays. Instead, he grabbed the seat he had used before and moved it to within a foot of Meg. Lifting with a puff and a grunt, he rocked slightly back to balance its weight on his modestly protuberant belly. In her surprise at the ease with which he did this, she snapped the piece of grass she held. Her wonder stirred Ekaterina to comment.

"Jackanapes is much stronger than he looks, you know. That's his dvarsh heritage manifest. He's carried you like a child's doll twice now." A teasing twinkle sparked across her eye. "Too bad he lacks some other qualities of the dvarsh."

Jack rose to the bait.

"What might those be, Cousin?"

"Well...you have an elf's restraint and a human's patience, for just two examples. Which is to say precious little of either."

"Now, Kate—" he started back.

She cut him off with exasperation.

"My name is not Kate! Why you persist in this humanish practice of affectionate diminutives is beyond me. I will thank you kindly to call me by my full and appropriate Ekaterina."

Momentarily hangdog, a more abashed figure than Jack Plenty was unimaginable.

"Ah, Cousin," he rejoined in a wounded tone. "Don't get hot. You know I think you're grand and great and a credit to the struggle. I wasn't meaning any disrespect. Besides," he straightened assertively, "I am some human, you know. A piece. A chunk. There's good in humans, too, like you always say, so there must be some good in some human ways, right?"

Ekaterina shrugged, looked at her nails and said nothing.

As Meg listened to the exchange her mind was actually elsewhere, trying to think of a tactful way to raise a question about their intentions. In Jack's last statement she saw her opening. Tossing aside the broken stalk of grass, she picked another, this one greener. She looped it and began threading the ends in and out, forming a ring. When she spoke, it was casually. She did not, at first, lift her gaze from the work of her hands.

"Ekaterina?"

The dvarsh turned from Jack to the younger woman with a deliberately exaggerated good will.

"Yes, dear?"

"Jack says that you're a 'credit to the struggle'?"

Ekaterina reacted with something very near a sniff, but the same vanity that provoked her pique also made her unwilling to entirely dismiss the compliment.

"It was a generous phrase, Meg, although his motives for stating such are suspect at the moment."

"Ah, Cousin," Jack objected, a flamboyantly stricken look on his face. "What are you saying?"

"That perhaps you chose your words with an eye toward sliding around trouble."

"But, Cousin. You know I hold you in the highest regard."

"Jackanapes." Ekaterina leveled her gaze on him. "I have no doubt of it."

"Well," Meg broke in, grimacing with the effort required to form her question in a way that satisfied her. "He's probably more right than just kind when he says it. I mean, I hope you're on my side and not against me, but..." she paused, "I'm not sure what you're struggling for. I know you say people think the wrong way about God, and what you say about that makes sense. And I know that all this killing and war and...and...," she groped for the word, "...exploiting people is sickening..."

"Just the fact of it nearly killed you," Jack interrupted, "killed your dad outright. Probably his Diné blood. You know, Navajo. He was a full quarter Diné, and his grandma had some influence. Laid him bare to the horror of it all."

"Jackanapes!" Ekaterina matched the edge of her tongue to the edge of her glare. "Do not interrupt. Meg is trying to ask us something important."

"It's okay, Ekaterina. Jack says things in a weird way but a lot of it is kind of helpful. I guess being a little bit Navajo helped make me sick, too."

"And West African," Jack interrupted again.

"What?" Meg jerked as if hit by lightning, her grass ring falling forgotten.

"African. Your West African blood. From your mother."

"Jackanapes, please be still!" Losing patience, Ekaterina slapped her leg. She addressed Meg more quietly. "It's true, dear. Your mother's line was enriched by West African genes. Yoruba for the most part, we documented. It is from your four-times great grandmother, a daughter of Xango, that you get many of your tendencies of mind."

"You're saying I'm part Negro?"

Meg's voice was dramatically flat. Jack's, responding, was not.

"'Negro!' What kind of word is that?"

"It's the proper word. It's the polite word," she shot back.

"Meg, dear, listen." It was now Ekaterina's turn to break in. "'Negro' is a word used by slave masters and conquerors. I know it is considered polite in quarters of your society right now, but in your lifetime that will change. You must help to do that. May I suggest you try 'African-American?'"

"African-American?" Jack chimed. "That's rather long in the mouth, Cousin. As often as not I'll bet your African-American is just Black in her own mind."

"There are varying degrees of consciousness in all phases of culture, dear boy. That follows from the eighteenth expostulation of 'pataphysical socionomics."

"I don't know consciousness from confectioner's sugar," he retorted, "But in Rome I can Roman with the best of them over rice and beans and a cup of joe. And I'll tell you that a word's got to feel alive in the mouth before it can fire the mind. Otherwise, the fuel's too rich and your brain will diesel. See what I'm saying?"

"Jackanapes, you're starting to frighten me," Ekaterina said curtly. "You seem to forget the first precept of changing the world is—"

Jack broke in, "First you have to change yourself. I do recall, sweetie. Some days, though, I do get hungry to let the p's mind the q's and myself commit to some serious basking."

"I had no idea. She never told me."

Meg spoke quietly, but a plaintive note sounded in her voice. Ekaterina's lips tightened and she shook her head before responding.

"As you know, your mother was of what is known as a Southern family, and such things are not talked about in what you call the South. She may not even have known. At the same time, it is exceedingly rare to find a so-called White Southerner with no trace of African blood. In four generations it will be hard to find anyone born on this continent who has not been improved by the mix." Her voice softened and hope colored her face. "A land of mestizo nations, creoles, metis, some pretending to nonexistent purity   "

"Improved by the mix!" Jack repeated. "Improved by the mix!"

"I just...it's just...well, you know what people think," Meg stammered. "And how do you know so much about me?" she added defensively.

"Hybrid vigor!" Jack shouted. "I love it. I love every shake-it-up drop of it!"

"Jackanapes, be silent!" Ekaterina commanded. "My dear," she began to Meg, "We know because we need to know and so we find out. You are not the first of any of your ancestral lines to have known us, and before us were others familiar to your kin. Your society is particularly free and stupid with the stigmas it attaches so you learn this as something of a shock. Unfortunately, in this consensus there are no records you can consult that could teach you more of your varied heritage. That notwithstanding, it makes you very special. A part of what makes you so important to us or, rather, would have made you important if you had consented to our request, is the specific genetic mix you embody. Not just for us, but for several lineages you could have been a...a Trojan horse. But these are no longer our concerns. I believe you were trying to ask about the nature of our ongoing struggle."

"Ye-es. Um. Yeah. I mean, I'd just like to know..."

"What we are trying to accomplish?" Ekaterina finished for her.

"Yes, what you are trying to accomplish."

"We are trying to save life. Dvarsh, thrm, human, they are all bound together, and they teeter on the brink of extinction." The broad, brown woman settled herself more firmly onto her section of log and continued, "Humans, your people, are the problem. Humans and their so-called technological development. Not just their powerlust and violence, but their petroleum, their coal, their logging and industrial farms, and especially their breeding. Humans breed like rats, but do to their world a great deal more destruction. And rats, in the wrong environments, are very destructive."

"Cousin," Jack chimed in, "Don't, you know, paint too rosy a picture or anything."

Ekaterina ignored him.

"Between human breeding and industrial farming and petroleum and constructing and chasing around there is no more silence. There is no more dark. The soil is being poisoned—and the air and the water. Horrible, nasty, accumulating poisons drive hordes and hordes of terrifying machines, planes and cars and cannons. None of which is the worst. The worst has not yet come."

"Do you really have to go into all the unpleasant details at just this moment?" Jack implored.

Ekaterina continued to ignore him.

"Even now servants of the War Beast are coming together in a windy place by the side of a contaminated lake. They are aided and abetted by minions from the criminal colony of Nemus Ilex on the western coast. These are terrible intellects your people have wrapped in fool's cloth of honor and virtue. Their intention is to unleash a killing force locked in the heart of stone and a poison that works for ten thousand years. This is one side of their project. There is another."

"I hate this part!" cried Jack. "I can't stand when you remind me!"

Ekaterina lowered her voice and leaned conspiratorially forward.

"They intend to make people's very appetites the next weapon of uncountable destruction. They intend that your people will lust themselves into oblivion in front of little boxes of changing light. Addictive light. A light that makes you feel like you live a life, when all you really do is eat what the light tells you to eat and squirt pee and pump poo. And watch the changing light."

"Aauuggh!" Jack shouted. "Stop! It's too terrible to stand!"

"Jackanapes." Ekaterina fixed him with her sternest glare. "Contain yourself."

"I don't think I understand that," Meg insisted. "How can you lust yourself into oblivion?"

"Oh, easily," Ekaterina answered. "The lust is for things, possessions. The weapon turns on the nature of possessions, the fact that every possession you own consumes a part of you. Tools, instruments, if they are more than conceits, these things do not defy the rule but they are exceptional enough they don't activate the weapon. Consequently, the mission of these alleged scientists is to create generalized lust, a frenzied lust for things unconnected to any sense of utility."

Jack leapt up and intoned,

> *"You'll pay, and they'll grind your sorry butt to dust*
> *with cheap sights packaged and priced to go*
> *like lozenges that excite a great hunger, lust*
> *for the raree, the glimpse of naked tit, the peepshow.*
> *Dammit, dammit, dammit, to hell and gone. Alas!"*

Ekaterina was silent for a moment after he finished. When finally she spoke it was while looking at her hands.

"This is our struggle: to re-bury the coal and slow the flow of petroleum from the earth," she counted them off from pinky to thumb on one hand, "To teach the farming way that cleans the soil and enriches the land. To bring the lore of machines run by energy of grass and waters and sun and wind. To place the love of silence and darkness again beside the love of noise and light. And to cause humans to greatly slow their breeding and breeding and breeding and breeding. This is our struggle." She leaned forward, hand up, the first two fingers loosely pointing to an unseen view. "If we fail, the planet will grow sterile and your people will die in hunger, thirst and waves of plagues. Our people and the thrm'm will die more slowly because the poisons here will render us unable to conceive. The skies will cease to be blue, the land will lose its verdure and the seas, well, the seas will be the first to go. Anything that does survive will be broken, mutant, discontinuous from us and mutually exclusive. It will be the new life of a shattered world, a world for chitinous, crawly things, not one for soft and tender emotion. I hope, child, I have answered your question."

Meg said nothing. None of it made sense, but she still felt an urge to deny it, deny it, even though Ekaterina's strange, rolling words carried a ring of truth. Suddenly, the autumn chill cut through all her layers of bundling wraps. She could not stop shivering.

# Twenty

ר o

"OTHER THAN THE TIME YOU SAW icandy, have you seen anything else you've been unable to explain?"

Meg sat with her legs extended, her feet resting on the mound of her father's grave. She stiffened noticeably at Ekaterina's question. Her gaze repeatedly slid away from the other woman's inquiring look, dancing across the late season's tiny, faded asters to roll up and fix on the point where a fir overtopped the aspen. She coughed, using a hand to cover her mouth.

"Meg, what were the other things you saw that you could not explain?" the dvarsh prompted.

With a sigh that was almost a moan, Meg confronted the other's waiting eyes. Sharply drawing a new breath, she answered in two short bursts. First, "I saw Jack two times that he says never happened." Then, "Is that what you mean?"

Ekaterina leaned forward, peering into the tense face before her. She looked searchingly at an expression grown stubborn.

After a moment, she asked, "You saw Jackanapes two times doing what?"

"Not the same thing both times," Meg answered.

She described the two scenes that worried her still, dwelling in detail on the unnaturalness of the world in which she was sure she had awakened. Jack's denial of the events she recounted in fewer words. Ekaterina listened intently, eyes aglitter. She heard Meg through before raising a question.

"The leaden heaviness you felt, it emanated from Jackanapes?"

Meg screwed up her forehead in concentration as she checked her memory.

"Yes. That's the way it seemed."

Ekaterina drummed her fingers on her leg.

"The device he used for smoking, you say it had two parts to the body, an upper and lower?"

"Yes," the human nodded. "And he poured something into the bottom. And whatever he smoked he took out of the top part."

Ekaterina drummed her fingers first on her leg, then her cheek.

"What was this device made from?"

"Glass. He called it 'opalescent,' which I think isn't too far off."

Meg watched in silence as Ekaterina mulled over this information. The younger woman was relieved to be taken seriously, especially as she did not herself know how to think about these experiences.

Ekaterina suddenly sat up straight and slapped her lap.

"Meg, you said my cousin was composing a poem. Could you repeat it or tell me what it was about?"

Meg knitted her brow trying to recall.

"I didn't really listen that much to the words."

"I know. One doesn't. But this is important, dear. Can you remember anything at all about it?"

"Well. He called his pipe a 'Chaldean chalice.'" She squinted as she willed herself to remember. "He said it was made of 'opalescent glass.' But the poem really seemed to be about that fiber you both use for spinning. He called it a gift, and then he said something about communion. And then he decided to smoke his pipe." She blew noisily through pursed lips and faced her companion directly. "When I describe it, it all sounds pretty weird, I know." A defensive edge entered her voice. "But you could see Jack doing all the things that I said, couldn't you? Couldn't you?"

"Alas, yes. Many times over. But this time? I'm not sure. We need him here."

For an instant, the dvarsh's eyes seemed to roll up into her head, her eyelids to droop. The expression passed before Meg was sure that she had seen it.

At a shouted, "On the way!" she looked up to see Jack rounding the cabin from the front, where he had been out of sight—presumably in the throes of thrmic transport. He adjusted his clothing as he hurried up the grade toward them.

Ekaterina allowed him to reach them and take a seat before she spoke. Settled onto a section of log, he placed his hands on his hips and waited. Ekaterina smoothed the lap of her garment and addressed him.

"Jackanapes. Meg has been telling me about some interesting experiences she has recently had."

"Not many experiences she's had on that cot, the pot nor the stump there where she sits," Jack responded.

His cousin favored him with an indulgent smile and continued, "Experiences of a kind possibly related to her 'icandy' visualization."

"Oh, right. Those cantankerous maxi-mojo shakings you told me about."

He spoke to his fist as to Yorick's skull.

"Spontaneous hallucinative lucubrations," Ekaterina corrected. "Really, dear boy, I have the impression sometimes that you do not pay attention."

"Wrong!" Jack sat up looking hurt and earnest. "Experiences. We're talking about Meggily Meg's mystical, mysterious, metamathemagical humannoying experiences. I'm Johnny-on-the-spot. I'm rapt attention. I'm entirely ears."

He gripped his knees and leaned eagerly forward.

"She said..." Ekaterina paused, fighting to keep her expression solemn. A smile almost won. "She said that in addition to the visualization she has had other experiences that seem to me quite possibly related. An interesting fact is that these others involve you."

"Me?" Jack asked, unbelieving.

"You," Ekaterina affirmed. "And she said that when she mentioned them you claimed to have no idea what she was talking about."

Jack ducked his head and cocked an eyebrow, his expression as dubious as any Meg had ever seen.

"Just what experiences would these be, Cousin?" he challenged. "Fever had her more than once confused, I recollect."

"For one, she says she woke one night to find you standing on a chair, naked, tumescent and wiggling your fingers at her. She gave an exact description of gravito-voluntary impassional amplification, and she says her sheets were being pulled slowly down without you touching them."

Jack's mouth fell open, his jaw so slack it rattled when he shook his head as though clearing his thoughts. He seemed, for a moment, to have lost his voice. When he found it his words were colored with indignation.

"Me do the Bah-rool seduction with the missy here? What are you asking me?" He jumped from his seat and threw his arms earnestly wide. "It's a poor way you have of kidding!" He dropped his arms and shrugged. "Don't get me wrong, but why would I stoop to that?"

"Would you stoop to that, Jackanapes?" Ekaterina asked.

"Cousin!" His hand went to his breast. "Cousin, you wound me! To protect and serve, right? To protect and serve! I gave my word before you went off! Didn't I? Didn't I?"

He paced a few steps forward and back, jaw thrust in advance. He halted and again threw his arms wide, but seemed to lose energy midway through the gesture.

"Besides," his arms dropped, "what fun is the Bah-rool if the other party can't beam back? The whole rush is the float through space on the tense, equally shivering wants of mutual projections. You know?"

"Exactly so, dear boy." Ekaterina reached out and patted his hand. "It does take on a rather different tone when it is not fed by the weight of two sets of expectations."

"And another thing!" Jack cried. "If a person's thirsty, do you think he, meaning me for instance, is going to a crystal spring or a chamber pot?"

"Excuse me?!" Meg checked him, indignation ready to enter her voice.

"Wait a minute." Jack's head sank turtle-like to his shoulders. "That didn't come out like I meant it."

"Take your time," Ekaterina advised. "Tell us what you actually mean."

He reddened deeply.

"It's just, you know. Here I am in the company of a number of very healthy and reasonably clean thrmish women who like Jack Plenty plenty. No offense, please, ma'am, but I didn't even much relish changing that diaper."

"So I noticed," Ekaterina said dryly.

"Well, Kate, I mean Cuz-ah, Kuh, 'Katerina..."

"Control yourself, Jackanapes."

"Right." He nodded solemnly, his guilty look softening the attitudes of both women. "Yeah, I was kind of crummy on the serve part. But she kept waking up and asking questions. Which I answered. And I did pretty well on the protect part, right?"

"So well that you scared her into the path of a bear."

"I was grabbing some sleep!" Jack shot back, visibly upset. "She couldn't even walk when I set to doze."

Ekaterina considered this for a moment.

"You are right, Jackanapes. You did as well as you could in those circumstances."

She drummed her fingers on her cheek some more.

"But in the present circumstances we must still conclude that Meg experienced a coercive form of the Bah-rool at the hands of one Jackanapes Plenty."

Ekaterina sat quietly for another thoughtful pause, then began in a soft voice, almost as if to herself, "We look at our evidence—the paralysis, the apparent glow in his eyes, the aura, the lurking forms never seen but remembered, and particularly the garish color combination of orange and gold—these things suggest at the least a somewhat unordinary kind of wakefulness."

She pondered some more, then went on, "On the other hand, she clearly saw Jackanapes Plenty, Bard of the Rigidstick, my cousin, engaging in a corrupt form of a practice of which she should have no knowledge."

"A corrupt form?" Meg blurted. "You mean there's some way to do it that's supposed to be okay?"

"Oh, sure," Jack answered. "Between two like-thinking individuals it's the greatest. When the moment ripens you drift through space to the juicy conjoin." He winked. "Shuddering bliss. You should try it next time."

"Next time?" Meg was emphatic "I've never tried any of it at all."

"Never?" Jack asked, his struggle to absorb this fact obvious in his rapid blinking. "Really?"

"Really," she snapped.

"Say..." Inspiration began to spread over his face. "Say, have you ever given much thought to unicorns? As possible working associates, that is."

"Jackanapes, you are off the subject."

Ekaterina had risen and was looking down her nose at him, hands on her hips.

"Um, sorry, Cousin. It just occurred to me how rare it is to find someone qualified..."

Jack's voice trailed off as Ekaterina's gaze sharpened. He made himself a picture of unobtrusive attention.

"The conclusion we come to," said Ekaterina, returning to her seat and her line of reasoning, "is that Meg did experience a coercive form of the Bah-rool at the hands of one Jackanapes Plenty. But probably not you, Jackanapes Plenty."

"Excuse me?" Meg asked, dismay in her voice.

"She means," Jack said, "That something happened with some Jack Plenty but not this Jack Plenty."

"Is there another one?"

"Multitudes," He answered. "Inevitably."

"Inevitably," Ekaterina repeated.

The young woman brimmed with frustration.

"Well, which one stood on the chair and wiggled at me?" she demanded.

"We can rule out a strictly paranoid delusion," Ekaterina answered, "because that would not have provided you with details of the Bah-rool. Even if we choose to think of this as a dream of waking we must admit that knowledge of these particular details suggests an additional perception. It could have been projection, some entire other phenomenon that you constituted as Jackanapes—"

"Same problem with the Bah-rool as with paranoia," interrupted Jack.

"Oh, yes. Right." Ekaterina nodded. "So, even if we are talking about a psychological state, it unquestionably involves some type of clairvoyance in its constituency."

"May as well start with the clairvoyance," Jack suggested.

"We may as well start with the clairvoyance," Ekaterina agreed, restoring her full attention to her two companions. "Go to the farthest point first and work back toward easy."

Before going on she again drummed her fingers on her cheek.

"There is another piece of evidence to consider, dear boy," she said finally.

"That icandy thing, Cousin? The visual-whatsit?"

"Visualization. One other besides that."

Jack leaned forward, intensity in his bearing. Ekaterina let her pause mature. Meg looked at her hands.

"Another episode in the company of another you."

"Heavens to Betsy!" Jack exclaimed. "I'm ramifying. Was I clad or jaybird bare in this one?"

"Clad," Meg informed him. "I remember definitely clad. You were wearing a very short wrap-around skirt."

"Really?" Jack straightened. "A skirt?" He seemed to find the idea satisfying. "How did I look, little darling? Fetching, I hope."

"It was all so...so unfamiliar," Meg responded. "I suppose you looked okay."

"More than that," Ekaterina spoke, "she observed you composing a communion hymn."

"A song of the love feast. But commissions for those verses don't commence for, let me see, it's autumn now—"

"She heard you compose the hymn you offered two years ago."

"Two years ago? You mean the one that begins

*"The gift we spin and cord and weave and sew*
*and reshape some winter afternoon as cookies...."*

"Yes!" Meg cried. "Yes, that's it!"

"But I wrote that better than two years ago," Jack insisted.

"And she saw you smoking through Rotterman's bong."

"Holy smokes! The sacred chalice?"

Jack looked as though he had been struck.

"The pearly chalice," Ekaterina assured him. "She described the procedure to the last detail. There is no doubt she observed it somewhere. Sometime."

"But Old Pop broke the chalice nearly forty years ago and counting, remember? Almost before my beard had grown. And of late we've set the communion smoking by the whereside, anyway. How's she going to see that, just a girly still?"

Jack's inflection lost emotional color as he spoke, and he seemed to grow distracted, his attention withdrawing steadily to elsewhere. Meg was surprised to watch his pupils contract to tiny points and his breathing slow. From a pocket he drew his oracle dice, rattling them in his hand as he stood, almost absently, then squatted beside the stump and cast the small black solids.

"Precisely the question," Ekaterina said. "How did she see it. Could she be looking into parallel universes? It's a possibility. We should make a list. Or perhaps it was—"

"Transconsensuality," Jack said flatly.

"Oh, I don't think so," Ekaterina responded quickly. "Not transconsensuality. There has never been a single case recorded in any of the annals. It's more one of those intriguing theoreticals that occupy overstimulated students in after-hours cafes. Like perpetual motion."

"Transconsensuality definite on the human," Jack persisted. "It's dead-on intuition."

He pointed to the dice.

"The myriad stars twice and a bar on the cube."

Ekaterina gave him a prolonged scrutiny. She noted the preoccupation in his aimlessly wandering eyes, his appearance of listening to something somewhere else. Minutes elapsed. Finally, she said, "When you're right, you're right. It is, after all, theoretically possible."

"Theoretically, yep, that's the thing," Jack agreed.

"You're just going to take his word for it?" Meg balked. "Just like that? Doesn't he have to have evidence?"

"He's an intuit," Ekaterina soothed. "When an intuit has a dead-on intuition it is folly to contradict. You can see the authenticating distraction there on the dear boy's face."

But even as he was discussed Jack seemed to flow back into the local present. He scooped up his dice and pocketed them while rising.

"And the next theoretical thing," he went on, "is what are we supposed to do now?" He rolled his eyes and clicked his tongue at his cousin. "Call for a team of crack bureaucrats?" He bearded her. "Clerical support? A custodial force? Write a twenty year plan for seeing if she can pick out shapes on the cards in our researcher's pocket behind consensus number two?"

"Jackanapes, your jocularity is, at this time, misplaced," Ekaterina chided.

"Hey, Cousin. Tell me it's not standard practice, just like I said," he shot back.

"Only," she conceded, "in low-intensity phases of struggle. Present circumstances seem to me to argue for a lower research profile and a more direct engagement with the subject."

"I'm sorry to drag you back here," Meg interrupted. "But this is all new to me and I don't have any idea what you two are talking about. What is 'trance consensuality?'"

"No, dear," Ekaterina began, "Not 'trance consensuality,' 'Trans—'"

"That's it!" Jack shouted. "That's it! Trance consensuality!"

"What are you saying, Jackanapes?"

His cousin spun back to face him.

"Kate-ah, Ka-ka-cousin! Cousin! Ekaterina, I did it!"

"Did what, dear boy? What did you do?"

"I found one. I found a clue, just like you always wanted."

"A clue? What kind of clue?"

"To the intuition!"

He alternated between beaming at his kinswoman and chuckling into his hand.

"To what intuition?" asked Meg.

Ekaterina answered.

"To his intuitive recognition of the transconsensual nature of your experiences. But," she continued to Jack, "you will have to provide more explanation on this clue of yours. What precisely have you recognized?"

He shifted from foot to foot.

"It was that wrong word for the right, same sound. You know, 'trans/trance?' That one. That's it."

"That's the clue? 'Trance' for 'trans?' You're saying she enters the transconsensual condition through the medium of trance?"

"Fire! I wouldn't know anything about that, Ekaterina. You'll have to tell me after you get your philosophers into it. It's the pun I'm talking about. And how to intuit. Like you always said, if you only had a clue where I got some of these things. Remember?"

"Your intuition arises in some way like Meg's misunderstanding?"

"No!" he barked. "From! From her misunderstanding, Cousin. From it."

"But," Meg objected, "You had your intuition first."

"Negatory, friend. The pun was pre-existent. You not understanding on that point was laying in the situation."

"Do you mean latent in the situation?" his cousin suggested.

"The very same," Jack nodded solemnly. "It was what caused all these links to my intuitive gland."

"Causal links?" Ekaterina interpreted.

"Exactly," confirmed Jack.

"Could you elaborate a little in the interests of science?" she pressed.

"Meg here, little Christmas, already didn't understand before we said what we said, so it stood out and I could tell. So I said what it was."

"Stood out how?" Meg asked.

Jack's brow furrowed.

"I didn't get that part. Do you think it's important? I mean, one kind of spectacles is as good as another, right?"

"Perhaps another time." Ekaterina clasped his hand in one of hers and patted it with the other. "I'm sure you've uncovered an important first insight."

"Not to change the subject," Meg put in, "but could we talk about these things that happened to me?"

"Try not to think of these as things that have happened to you," Ekaterina offered. "Rather, think of them as the first trials of an interesting new ability."

"What kind of ability only happens when you're too weak to control it?" Meg retorted.

Jack mugged and grinned at her.

"Those are some of the very best," he said, giving her one of his exaggerated winks.

"Jackanapes! Enough!" Ekaterina admonished. Then, turning to Meg, she spoke with reassurance, "Think of the first sounds one produces on an unfamiliar musical instrument. But after a little practice, a little discipline, the zoot horn croons as well as belches and the violin's tonalities are made sweet. Perhaps you will find it evolves in a similar fashion."

"Cousin, excellent!" Jack shouted. "You made a poem!"

"Contain yourself," Ekaterina shot back. "We are having a discussion."

"I don't see how you can call it an ability," Meg resisted. "I mean, it hasn't happened because I wanted it to. I can't make it happen."

"Are you certain you cannot?" Ekaterina asked. "Events with the alternate Jackanapes occurred when your physical control was weakened by sickness, but your visualization of icandy came at a moment of deepest relaxation. A comfortable pallet and your imagination can duplicate the caresses of the Thrm."

"But say, Cuz, ah, Ekaterina," said Jack, "You know that is real choice, '...the zoot horn croons as well as belches and the violin's tonalities are made sweet.' You're a genius."

"Jackanapes, please let it go for now."

"All right," he responded. "But I might pop back home a little later and share it with everybody. I might even have to spin out a few variations. The Ekaterina variations. Variations on a poem by Ekaterina, elder of the Nondifferential Clan."

Her voice carried the full measure of her exasperation.

"Would you please join us in our conversation for a few minutes? I am not at this instant prepared to discuss an accusation of poetry."

He leaned back and looked away from her, but muttered, "Crooning zoot horn belches. Wow."

Meg stared at her hands, her whole face trying to concentrate between her eyebrows. She tapped her foot in a thoughtless gesture. In a moment she lifted her head and spoke to the small, brown woman before her.

"What does it mean that I have this 'ability?'"

"How the heck should we know?" Jack dismissed her question. "You're the only one that's ever been."

"Stay calm, dear," Ekaterina advised her. "And let one of us know immediately if it ever happens again."

"But," Meg objected, "please don't take offense, but how am I supposed to know which impossible, unexplainable things are reality and which aren't?"

Jack let out so tremendous a sigh that his body appeared to deflate as he exhaled.

"The whole of all we've been saying," he said, "is that it's every bit of it reality."

His tone softened some.

"Now here or there is altogether different. That, I'll give you, is a matter of opinion."

# *Twenty-one*

THE NEXT DAY MEG AND EKATERINA were again sitting beside the grave of Mr. Christmas. Despite brilliant sun enriching the reds and golds of well-turned leaves, the light breezes crossing their somewhat protected spot carried a hard edge that promised snow soon and the rest of winter's train. Meg knew that in the lands below, autumn was not so far advanced. There were, she thought, a thousand things about those lands that were not so far advanced as in this remote meadow where her father lay beneath a modest berm. She tried to picture herself with friends from school, carrying on about the war, and boys and future plans, little scandals, all the things on the radio. She could not make the image come clear. That world no longer seemed entitled to the same measure of credence as this one where Ekaterina deftly twirled her spindle and a whole tribe of thrm'm—old, young and all ages between—alternated tending to her and conceiving their next generation. The realm in which she had lived her entire past felt less substantial than this one where the funny hybrid Jack talked his peculiar talk that sounded like his mind did no editing, shouted his poems, sported with the Thrm or did Ekaterina's bidding. Or sometimes, like now, just disappeared.

She scanned the meadow to see if he was copulating among the elves who had spilled out of the cabin unmindful of the briskness in the air. She was almost used to their ecstatic frenzies, used enough that she could note the individual contours of their small, beautiful bodies, the differing ways they hiked their skirts or clung—often even in the throes of orgasmic transport—each to her or his hardwood staff.

She saw Sweetheart moving in a tangling cluster, caressing and jabbering in the non-stop, thrm'mic way. Occasionally, another elf would shove its head under Sweetheart's shawl in order to suck a swallow or two of the special milk. Ekaterina estimated the elf woman would continue this precious lactation for another two years before her metabolism changed again and allowed one of the sperm she carried cached and cocked within her womb to make her pregnant. Meg was somewhat jealous at the sight of those others taking the liquid that was bringing her own body back to health, but her dvarsh friend had told her that sharing this drink was a necessary part of the life of their kind, and she knew from watching that they really took very tiny sips. Nevertheless, she felt some satisfaction at noting a second woman had apparently just begun to give the milk and that Sweetheart was no longer alone in suckling her kin. Both of these thrm'm went often to Ekaterina, who applied a salve to their nipples to minimize the chafing from too many pairs of even these gentlest lips.

Meg looked more intently for Jack, hoping to see him step back into this world, if, indeed, he had traveled into another consensus and not just into the woods to fatten (like the bear she had startled) on honey and leftover berries. For reasons she could not explain to herself she desperately wanted to witness one of these transpossible arrivals. The day of the wolf's visit Ekaterina had used her cloak to hide the actual moment of consensual departure. From it she had learned only that the consensual jump was at once quieter and less electrically active than the spatio-temporal shift of General Rataxes. The strength of her desire to witness the act stopped just short of pushing her to ask for a demonstration.

She wondered if they appeared all at once, like a pop, or in quick succession, as though stepping through a doorway.

Ekaterina hummed softly beside her, her own eyes commanded by the dance of fiber and twist of the spindle.

Meg was scanning the edges of the meadow when she jerked back with a gasp, nearly falling from her seat she was so startled. Standing in the shadow of the trees closest to the cabin she saw a figure staring fixedly at her. At first she thought it was a bear on its hind legs but, no, she told herself, it was too humanlike. Then she thought it might be a man in bear skins, but the pelt seemed to be the creature's own. And it was too impossibly tall. And, even at that distance, in some distinct way non-human.

"Ekaterina...," she began.

"Don't worry, dear. He'll approach when he's ready." She never looked up from her spinning. "His kind are ever reticent about contact. A good trait in a world spilling over with humans."

"What...what is...he?" the younger woman stammered.

"We call them H'yeth'ti, which translates to your tongue as something like 'sages' or 'the profound ones.' They call themselves . . . 'Er'rrggh,'" Ekaterina made a sound like a low groan sung through chewing. "Your kind call them various things. Sasquatch. Big Foot. In Asia, Yeti. Which is really a corruption of our word, you know. They are very, very private people. And, quite possibly, the deepest of all thinkers."

This seemed too incongruous a statement for Meg to let pass.

"You're telling me Big Foot may be the deepest of all thinkers?"

The challenge in her tone was obvious, but the other was unfazed.

"Oh, yes. Their powers of observation are extraordinary. They miss nothing. They may brood for days on the fine points of implications with which we may have only just begun to wrestle. Or of which we may even be unaware. It's not often that they meet with us, but whenever they do it is a kindness. I would bet that he brings news of other humans."

Meg suddenly chilled to the bone. She had not really wanted to think about meeting her own kind so soon. She felt she was only beginning to glimpse the truth of the world, and she felt alone in this of all the teeming millions of her species.

"Ekaterina..." she began.

"Yes, dear?"

"Ekaterina..."

"Yes?"

"I don't know, Ekaterina. I don't..."

At this moment Jack stepped from behind a tree near the Sasquatch and held his hand out toward the creature. The giant sniffed at the offered hand, both back and palm. Then he turned deliberately and urinated on the tree by which he stood. Jack dropped to all fours and sniffed at the spot, let out a laugh, jumped up and slapped the Sasquatch on the back. He then grabbed the creature's hand and began to lead him toward where the two women sat, talking to the great creature in a steady stream as he tugged him along.

As they came into earshot Meg heard him saying, "...knew your younger sister, too. Met her when she was weaning her second one, you know. Fine intuit, she is. Taught me a few of the subtler aspects of the jump. Always been grateful for that. Hope you'll convey my respects next time you meet her, in this realm or another. And those nippers of hers, I'll bet they're big as houses by now. I'll bet they're into all the berries. I'll bet—"

"Jackanapes! Do be quiet before you bore him to discorporation."

The sternness in Ekaterina's voice somehow still conveyed indulgence.

"Please bring him forward for a proper introduction."

"We're on the way, Ka...Kah, ah, Cousin. Coming just now with a skip and a whistle."

And, as good as his word, Jack renewed his grip on the creature's hand while spicing the air with a trilling tune.

The greeting between Ekaterina and the Big Foot was as curious as any Meg had ever seen. She looked back and forth from the pelted giant to the dvarsh in their curious dress, thrm'm in the background, and marveled at the ordinariness with which these beings inhabited her landscape.

Jack made awkard but adequate enough introductions, beginning, "Sir, allow me to present my cousin and comrade, Ekaterina Rigidstick, Thirty-three and a Third Magnitude Exemplary Metamathemage of the Nondifferential Clan. Cuz, this is..." and he uttered a long series of rising and falling belched grunts through which his tongue somehow steadily fluttered, concluding with, "I knew his Dad that year I summered in the far pass. Also did a bit of advanced study with one of his sisters," adding nervously, "Nothing recreational, you understand. Strictly job related.

"Oh, yeah," he added, indicating Meg, "This is our human. She's not so bad."

For a moment the creature craned its head forward, sniffing in the human's direction, noisily pulling air deeply into his lungs. He seemed reluctant to approach her more closely than within several feet. Turning to Ekaterina, he addressed her with a kind of articulated exhalation approximately crossing a protracted sigh with a sustained groan. A variously percussive grunting did the work of consonants.

Ekaterina translated, "He greets us all as distant cousins, 'earth people around the circle,' as they say of the lot of us. And he says that you, dear, don't smell quite as bad as most of your kind."

She then replied to him in his own language, beginning a long exchange that involved a number of manual gestures as well as peculiar vocalizations. Jack, as usual, interrupted now and again with comments in English or H'yeth'ti or Dvarsh, whatever seemed to be wandering through his mind. Ekaterina and the stranger would listen politely, but neither seemed to pay any real attention to him. After a while he was distracted by a red leaf dancing in the wind. He disappeared in pursuit of it, jumping and grabbing and egging himself on with whooping yells and shouts of encouragement.

Meg studied the creature before her as he talked with her companion.

He was, she decided, over seven feet tall, with most of that in his trunk. His legs did not look much longer than her own. His arms, on the other hand, were quite long and joined to shoulders of impressive breadth. He had prominent brows and a high crown, and a face that was somewhere between a human and an ape. His pelt was a deep reddish brown with some gray around his mouth and down his back, and covered him everywhere except on his upper face and ears, belly, crotch and buttocks, his fingers and toes, the palms of his hands, the soles of his enormous feet. His every movement was marked by a kind of ponderous grace, his face by a wider range of expression than any Meg would ever have imagined. She thought his smell the most surprising thing. Not at all thick or musky as she might have imagined, but pleasant, almost spicy.

He and Ekaterina seemed to suddenly conclude their conversation and he turned and spoke directly to Meg.

"He wants to know if he can touch your hair," Ekaterina translated.

Meg cringed involuntarily, but nevertheless managed to give him a weak smile and nod. He stepped closer and gently fingered a hank, then lightly stroked her left cheek, traced the line of her jaw to her chin. Withdrawing his hand, he tilted his head and regarded her for a moment in silence, spoke again to Ekaterina, gestured to her a sign that involved both of his large, heavy hands, walked away into the woods behind where the women sat, and was gone.

Meg was straining to catch a glimpse of him through the trees when she realized Ekaterina was staring at her.

"What's the matter?" she asked.

"Forgive me, child. I was just thinking about what he said in parting," the dvarsh answered.

"What did he say?"

"He said that you are very soft and pretty for an agent of death."

Meg heard this statement with much chagrin.

"Agent of Death? How could I be?"

"I believe he meant not just you, but humans. His kind have taken more losses than even the Dvarsh. Every year to your kind they lose more of the only places for which they are adapted to live."

The younger woman digested this explanation.

"He's someone I'll never ever see again, isn't he?"

Ekaterina gave her half a smile.

"Now, I'm not competent to give judgment on that. But probably not if you cleave to the human way, sweet child. Not as a daughter of rapacious men. But come. He brought news that must stir us all to action. Tomorrow they will be here to take you out of the mountains. Jackanapes and I must gather the thrm'm and be gone."

Ekaterina started down the slope toward the cabin, but Meg sat as if fixed to her seat, feeling her warm tears chill as the breeze dried them on her face.

# Twenty-two

## 22

IT WAS THE SUDDEN STILLNESS IN the cabin that woke Meg next morning. All the low chuttering and wrrs, the rustling and shuffling, the many patterns of breathing abruptly stopped. She sat upright on her cot with a start, her glance darting right and left around the room, ears straining. She was, at first, disoriented, unable to fix on the cause for her waking. From outside she heard the wind's light sough and the piercing call of a jay in the first light. Inside the cabin all was still. Everything she could see from her bed seemed neat and ordered, in its place. Motes drifted languorously, unperturbed in the beams breaking under and around the sash on the east facing window. The cabin looked exactly as it should have, and she sensed no threat or concern from outside. Then she realized they were gone.

Entirely gone. Meg rose from the bed and dressed quickly, grabbing without thinking a very human plaid shirt and dungarees. She checked both rooms thoroughly, but found no evidence Jack, Ekaterina, or the Thrm had even been there. The elves had never touched much more than the floor of the cabin—except her bed and herself—but even those items used by the two dvarsh were returned to precisely the spots from which they originally had been taken. She became acutely aware of the solitude.

Completely alone at this mountain station was something she had never experienced. For the last—what was it? ten days? a week? two weeks? more? less? no more than three weeks maximum, she was certain, and less than that she felt—Meg had lived in company of beings who seemed now like lost members of her own family. She was still alive because of care they had lavished, and the world she saw through brimming eyes had been forever enlarged to include these new, abruptly departed branches of her line. To include also a breadth and depth now yawning around her but perceived only dimly, and closed to her access by the cabin's sudden emptiness. She sank into a chair under the weight of her sense of abandonment.

And her father was dead. Her father! She remembered it with a shock, almost as though the fact were new at that moment. With dismay she thought of the last several days in which she had passed long hours beside his grave, steeped in the rare, rich sun gracing the deepening autumn of the high elevations. It seemed to her she had felt no grief for him, or even herself at his passing. A sadness, yes, that he would speak to her no more, and a regret she had never had the chance to ease his worry for her or his fear that he was insufficient as her single parent. He had constantly felt the lack of too few resources and too few opportunities, but he had been smart and kind, awkwardly gentle, determined to do everything in his power to open for Meg all the doors he had found barred. Sitting beside his grave with Ekaterina she had felt him still with her, still present and living, if fleshless in this chunk of pluralistic reality. In the stillness of the cabin, the vapor of her every exhalation clearly visible in the unwarmed air, she was stricken with guilt that he had been dead and buried for some uncounted days and she had not grieved for him. She had not mourned the person who had made his wishes, his needs, his happiness secondary to, conditional upon, hers.

"I love you, Daddy," she spoke to the room. The dam burst. Sorrow whelmed. She sobbed with her entire body. It did not seem she could stop.

Later, she sat drawn up in the rocking chair, hugging her legs to her chest, her chin resting on her knees, staring fixedly at nothing. She dwelt in a concrete, physical ache that was her body's response to her father's death. Still later she felt the call to visit the outhouse, and roused herself to address that need. Returning to the cabin, she realized she was hungry. Feeling a little ashamed for it, she ate lightly, enough only to allay the pangs. She built up the fire enough to take the chill off the room, then let it burn down. Her clean-up was overly particular.

By midmorning her breakfast crumbs were swept away and her utensils cleaned and stowed. She sat again in the rocker, moving little except to breathe and blink. Every detail of the cabin spoke to her of her solitude, her father's death, of abandonment by Jack and Ekaterina. She began to long for the sense of presence she had felt while sitting those last days beside her father's grave. Going into her trunk to get another sweater to layer beneath her coat she found the dvarsh clothing given her by Ekaterina, folded in a meticulous fashion that could only have been the work of that broad, nut brown woman. Remembering the hours she had passed warm and snug in the face of autumn's bite, Meg quickly changed into the dvarsh shawls and wraps, folding and stowing the human clothes she stepped from. Dressed thus she felt again connected, in slight degree, to the vanished others—dwarf folk, father, elves. She walked out of the cabin and up the meadow, to take one of the seats Jack had placed beside the grave.

Sitting there she became aware that some current of the sense of her father's presence really had remained with her. More fragile now, not to be taken for granted in the way she had taken it those last few days, the sense that her father still watched over and loved her was a tangible certainty. She cried again, the tears cold where the wind took them from her face, but more quietly this time, with no sobs and but few sniffles.

She had sat for a time liminally aware of the air's passage over her face and its song in the trees behind her, when her attention was drawn to movement down the meadow. Near the trees but advancing into the clearing, about midway between the meadow's lower end and the cabin, moving in fits and starts toward the latter, was a solitary thrm. From the flatness of its chest and the way it moved she thought it might be a male, but it was hard to be sure given the distance and the fact that most thrm'm carried similar staffs and all wore identical shawls and skirts.

This one seemed distressed. It would move quickly toward the cabin for a couple of yards, then stop, raise itself to its full height and look around, calling. The wrring trill that reached Meg was plaintive and questioning. In an instant she made out the berry stains around his mouth and knew this was Roamer, wandered out of range of the link when Jack and Ekaterina had taken the rest through the jump. An empath cut off from the rest of his emotional community, he was profoundly lost and alone in a way that made Meg think her own solitude trivial.

She rose, intending to go to him to soothe and calm. As she stood she glimpsed a more distant movement, this one on the trail rising to their station. Peering intently she was able to pick out men and mules and knew this was the party of which the Sasquatch had told, come to pack out her father and herself before snow rendered the high meadow unreachable.

It was only then she thought of the radio. In the normal course the watchers at the outposts used their short-waves to check in with their headquarters and with each other almost daily. Over the term of her illness and recovery her colleagues below would have tried to raise her father with increasing frequency, their concern growing as no answer came back from the mountain. Meg wondered that no one had come to investigate the silence earlier. Had they just been overlooked, she asked herself, or had the dvarsh used mysterious, unmentioned tactics to lull bureaucratic suspicion? The probable frame of mind with which these men approached began to worry her. She had a picture of them, edgy and unpredictable, climbing the trail fearful of what they would find.

From their position she realized that they would enter the clearing before she could reach the thrm and lead or carry him to cover. She knew without hesitation that she did not want Roamer taken or even observed by other humans. She was no longer even sure she wanted to be found herself without the protecting presence of Mr. Christmas.

She made a decision.

Drawing back to the edge of the trees she focused her attention on Roamer. Ekaterina had said that her kind drew the Thrm to them with deliberate love. Meg did not really know what that meant but she was determined to try to reach the elf with her emotions. She imagined holding him tightly to her, stroking him softly to calm his fear and speaking to him in soothing tones. With this image she beamed a pleading that was immoderate, continuous, "please...please...please...."

The effect on Roamer was immediate. He fell over, then jumped to his feet, seeming frozen in place. He stared straight at the spot where she lingered in shadow under the trees. She tried to put more urgency into the pleading, letting it well up and fill her mind. Roamer stood fixed, motionless. Involuntarily, her image of protecting and soothing him began to give way to fear. This seemed to bring him to life. He moved toward her.

His progress seemed to take forever. When he still had almost half the distance to cover she realized that he would not be safe before the men broke into the clear. Her heart began to sink. She saw the men coming to the mouth of the trail. She was desperate that they not even see him, and they had only to look up and there he would be. She knew if they saw the thrm they would hunt him, especially after finding the cabin apparently deserted and discovering the mounded grave. Hunting Roamer, they would find her and finding her they would have the thrm. What might happen to Roamer then she did not even want to think. She saw the lead man's head starting to come up from watching the ground where he stepped. She waited for him to see and call out. The lift of his head seemed to take an eternity. She could see most of his face.

"Hide him, hide him...."

While she concentrated on loving the thrm another part of her attention groped about, straining, trying to force something she was unable to conceive to happen.

"...hide him, hide him...," chanting again, trying to hammer a tocsin to her hidden nature. A ripple passed over the world. She reached within, achingly, for veiled powers, a secret gift for the heroic that she craved to locate. But the man's head still rose with incredible, unbearable slowness. Roamer, she loved him, would be discovered.

Without warning, the meadow rang with a horrific shriek. The mules brayed and kicked and broke free, shying from the men, who suddenly found their hands full. Roamer charged into her arms and she moved back farther into the trees.

It took Meg a second to sort out what had happened. The h'yeth'ti had leapt from behind a tree, shrilling like bloody murder, slapped the flank of the lead mule as it bolted across the trail, and disappeared into the forest on the other side. The result had been pandemonium among men and mules.

She held the little man tightly as she watched the drivers struggle for control of the animals. When at last they had them in hand, she sank to the ground under some covering juniper, in a position that would allow her to watch the clearing while she and the thrm remained undetected. Roamer clung to her trembling. She stroked his back and the back of his head, and spoke to him in soft, low tones she hoped would calm him. He burrowed into her clothes until she could feel the pounding of his heart and the hot panting of his fright against her skin. She held him and talked to him and tried to emote feelings of safety. She wondered whether the fear that had grabbed him was from the Bigfoot's scream itself or from the icy lance it had thrust through her mind and heart. Not that it mattered. The thrm was safe if they could but remain unobserved.

# Twenty-three

AFTER THE MEN REGAINED CONTROL OF their mules they proceeded to the cabin. Obviously still spooked from their encounter with... they didn't know what, they came quietly, nervously, glancing every which way as they led their animals up the meadow. There was none of the laughter and loud calling for her father that had marked their arrival in years past. They said nothing at all until they stood close in front of Meg's low residence, then Nate Miller, always lead man on the pack team, called, "Christmas! Hey, there, Christmas!"

When there was no answer Nate and one of the others—Guy, she remembered, Nate's younger brother—each took a hunting rifle from among the packs on their respective mules and started toward the door. The cabin hid them from sight, but she knew that they must have taken positions on either side of the door. The third man, old Mr. Grayson—the only one of them she was disposed to trust—now held the reins to all three mules. He drew them around him and stooped slightly so that he was in the midst of and protected by the creatures. Meg knew the moment Nate and Guy entered the cabin by the way Grayson started looking to every side in a darting manner, half popping up above the level of the mules' backs, then dropping again when he realized that he was exposed.

Abruptly, he seemed to fix right on her, to stare directly into her hiding place. Her heart pounded as she tried to will herself into the earth without crushing the thrm. Then she realized that what Grayson saw was her father's grave.

He called for Nate and Guy.

Roamer had responded instantly when she stiffened at Grayson's sudden long look in their direction. The thrm's burrowing had taken him completely inside her loose, heavy dvarsh clothes so that he nestled against her bare skin. When fear of discovery went through her like a shot, he immediately began to stroke her with quick massaging touches to her belly, her side, what he could reach of her back. He accompanied these motions with a low, protracted, lulling wrr. No longer surprised by the effects of any ministrations of the Thrm, she merely noted that her heart-rate steadied without slowing, her breathing regularized and her fright seemed to retreat, leaving her the gift of heightened awareness.

She was still concentrating on Grayson and did not heed at first when Roamer's touches became more caressive. She did not notice he had fallen silent until he sang a short, interrogative trill. Her first reaction was surprise. Then she realized that what the thrm was doing felt good.

It felt very good.

Her heart began to beat hard again, and her breathing changed. Meg shifted slowly onto her back and drew her arms inside her clothing so that she might return the touches of the small ward of her directed love.

She found the rhythm of Roamer's movement and moved with him, using one hand to cup his buttocks and the other to stroke between his shoulder blades, slide into his mane. She breathed in and out with the pleasure, her body given in full to the good of it, but her mind to her own private surprise still stood off in a corner, uninterfering but watching this happen to her, watching herself happen in this.

From her reading she knew the ways and means of repro-duction; however, no source available to a curious teen-aged woman had told her any part of it could feel so good. Roamer's intimacies were worlds more delicious than her self-explora-tions, and incomparably more satisfying than the once or twice high school boyfriend's lunging grope. Someone should have told her about the good feeling part. Someone should have told her about the richness of the good. Later she would resent this.

She was completely unprepared for what happened next. Over a matter of seconds the intensity of the sensations mounted, building and building until it seemed more than she could contain, and then it burst, expanding through her and out, washing through her, her love, the air about them, the ground on which she lay. One, tiny percussive sound forced itself through teeth she had clamped against the need to cry out. Her back arched and her legs stiffened. She rose on her shoulders and heels for a pulsing moment and then dropped again flat on the ground. Allowing herself a single, muted sob, she clasped Roamer tightly as she rolled onto her side in order to look out from her place in the shadows to check on the men.

Later she was going to think about a lot of things.

The three men were approaching her father's grave. Their voices were low and agitated and now all three carried guns. The first of them was nearly at the grave before she understood what they were saying.

"...tell you there wasn't a sign in the cabin." Nate was insistent. "Nothing to say where they are, but someone's been there as recent as yesterday, maybe this morning. There's still some warmth in the stove."

"What do you think of those tracks we saw around the door?" Guy asked. "Those...those monkey-thing tracks. Must've been a hundred of them. And that, ah, that bear—"

"That was no bear," Grayson broke in. "I'm not saying what it was, but a bear it wasn't."

"I think we found one of them," Nate said. "Like you thought, Gray. It can't be anything but a grave. I wonder if it's Christmas or the girl."

The three men stood beside the mound. They took in the sections of log fanned in a semicircular arrangement beside it. They looked at each other uncomfortably then back at the grave.

"There's just something not right about this—" Guy began.

Roamer suddenly let out a long chuttering sigh.

"What was that?"

Grayson's head jerked around and he stared into the shadows where Meg hugged the thrm to the earth.

"Don't start hearing things," Nate opined dryly.

"No, Nate," Guy objected. "There was something."

He lifted the barrel of his gun and took a couple steps toward the two in hiding. He peered long at the shadow under the brambled clump where they lay.

"So," Meg thought, "This is it."

Her reactions surprised her. Rather than being tensed to flee or fight, she was warm with resentment at this intrusion into the luxuriously relaxed embrace her body felt was its due. She continued to breathe slowly, deeply, regularly, almost silently as she looked out at the men who now crept slowly toward her. Deep in the back of her mind—infinitesimal and almost transparent—a living, evolving pattern seemed to flash on. It blinked dimly in a lower corner, as it were, of her awareness.

"Why not?" she whispered as she let go of her grounding assumptions. Her interior being dilated to accommodate the vining and sliding of the pattern as it permeated her sense of the world.

Through the pattern's dance she saw two men with guns edging toward her, a third looking on with weapon poised to fire. She visualized her love for the thrm as a radiance that flowed from her to him, and she reached into uncertainty.

Over all her senses came a doubling. All things around her seemed suddenly to be twice in themselves. Except, that is, for the men. She now saw two distinct sets of them, neither group entirely substantial, one in which Guy and Grayson continued to edge toward her hiding place, and another in which the men remained close together beside her father's grave. This second group peered uncertainly into the edges of woods around them, making no move to approach the limit of the clearing.

She heard a voice from this latter group, faint and tinny, "I really think you imagined it. You two 'fraidy cats."

"Hey, Nate," Guy whined in a muted buzz, "Better safe than sorry. You know, something is just plain weird up here."

She flowed toward this possibility, pulled her loving and the thrm along with her, until only a gossamer dust of an outline of beings remained in the shadow when the other Guy rushed the bramble under the bush and kicked at the accumulation of leaf matter and detritus beneath it. A tenuous Meg-shape had sprung away, disguised by the trembling of the bramble and by the rain of litter thrown up in Guy's sudden fury.

The almost invisible Meg shape stood off in the woods until Nate called, "I really think you imagined it. You two 'fraidy cats."

Frustrated and sheepish, Guy backed out of and away from the trees until Grayson reached to tap him so the two would not collide. They returned toward Nate in a sidewise fashion, more or less protecting each other's back.

"Hey, Nate," Guy whined, "Better safe than sorry. You know, something is just plain weird up here."

The fairy dust shape of Meg slipped back to lie again in the shadow of the juniper.

"Just shut up about it, why don't you," Grayson snapped. "Okay? Just shut up."

As the old fellow said this the two sets of humans merged again into one and she saw them as she saw the rest of the world, shimmeringly doubled within themselves, as if she viewed them simultaneously from two distinct but identical perspectives.

"Both of you!" Nate asserted his authority. "Give me some quiet. I've got to think a minute."

He looked deliberately around, appearing to memorize the scene. When his scrutiny was well past her bramble and scrap of shadow, Meg flowed back into and once more filled the scantly diaphanous form that had been both the relay and the beacon for what her heart told her was home.

"Should we, you know, ah, dig 'em up?" Guy asked.

Nate and Grayson both looked at him sharply.

"I mean, you know, shouldn't we take the body down to the coroner or something?"

Just then the air rang with a piercing, almost human but not quite human scream. Meg knew it for a reprise of the h'yethti's earlier alarm. It was enough for the three men.

Nate pointed to the sky where newly massing clouds promised an imminent change in the weather.

To Guy he said, "I don't think so. That was definitely not a cougar. And I predict we're going to see a real sudden cooling off and a whole lot of high mountain snow. Whichever one is in that hole will keep. I say let's leave everything be and get the hell off this mountain."

Grayson was already on his way to gather the mules.

# Twenty-four

MEG HELD ROAMER TIGHTLY TO HER with one hand and stroked him reassuringly with the other until well after the men had disappeared down the trail. At the breath in which she began to feel the safety of their absence, Roamer began again to caress and move against her in a way that spoke of his, and brought her again to, arousal. This time she quickly rolled onto her back to accommodate his movements as she consciously and deliberately loved the thrm with every fiber of her being. Ten, twenty, maybe even more years in the future, she would have a child. A different kind of child, perhaps one who would grow up to be great, or perhaps only to be different, but born of this joining. The shadow of a thought of its birth drifted at the edge of her mind, but her body was awash in the pleasure of Roamer's touch, and the love that fed him and held him close occupied the center of her expanding mind. She greeted her second orgasm with tiny, shrill noises that were but an echo of the bursting glee she felt—part joy in the fact itself, part the triumph of confirming that the first experience was not a danger dealt anomaly. In the aftermath she held him limply where he rode the rise and fall of her tranquil respiration. Against the soft flesh of her belly she felt his heartbeat slow over time from the rapid hammering patter that had marked his climax.

She was massaging the base of his neck and absently watching the fall of what she only slowly understood to be a first snowflake when she heard a sharp whistle and Ekaterina's shout from near the cabin. Reluctantly she sat up, still cradling Roamer against her. It was then she noticed the temperature had fallen considerably. Ekaterina called again, followed by a deeper boom from Jack. As she began to get to her feet Roamer started to struggle to get out from within her clothes, and she realized that Ekaterina and Jack must be summoning him with their more proficient affectional rays. The thought sent a pang through her which stopped Roamer instantly. He whimpered, and she knew he was torn between the love in which she held him and that which called from the two below. She quickly got him out from under her wraps and tousled his mane.

"Run on," she said. "I'm coming right behind."

Roamer burst into a trilling, ebullient song and bolted down the slope, bounding over her father's grave, a good foot's clearance in the passage. Meg followed more slowly, still giddy with new knowledge of possible sensations, with dimensions of consensual possibility.

When she got to the cabin Ekaterina had the wayward thrm in a bear hug. Jack stood by, somewhat awkwardly, patting Roamer on his head and shoulders. Tears flowed down Ekaterina's cheeks and she was talking in a way Meg had not heard her use before.

"I was so afraid for you," she said. "Those men with their guns and appetites, I didn't know what they would do to you. We left in such a rush I didn't even miss you at jump. I'm so sorry. I'm so sorry. Ekaterina would never want anything bad to happen to you."

"I found him," Meg said. "We hid together."

Ekaterina looked up at her with a grateful smile that turned immediately to sharp scrutiny.

"More than hid together, I think. No human gets that kind of glow from merely hiding."

Meg blushed deeply. Ekaterina grinned.

"Come here, child. Let me give you a hug. I had thought you would leave with the men."

"I probably would have, but there was Roamer. And I missed you. And...and they frightened me. A little."

"Come," the other woman repeated, "Give me a hug."

"Kate," Jack enthused, "I mean, I mean, Ekaterina. It's snowing! It's starting to really snow. Those conjectures of yours are absolutely doing the trick."

"Come inside," Ekaterina answered. "We have many les- sons to cover and only one slightly enhanced mountain winter for the learning."

The dvarsh woman bustled into the cabin, Roamer wrring and clicking and chuttering beside her. Meg paused and turned in the doorway. She stood watching as large flakes softened the view and began to flock the meadow's grass.

From where he stood in his declamative pose, himself rap- idly collecting a cover of white, Jack intoned:

> *"Out of the pot and into the flame,*
> *stepped the intrepid intuit,*
> *a human girl just come of age,*
> *a metamathemage*
> *and my little buddy, gathered, as we view it,*
> *for the sake of the project we engage,*
> *to the last extreme if we screw it,*
> *through one high winter our minds to tame*
> *...the future?*
> *We might get around to it."*

The End

# About the Author

ROBERT STIKMANZ IS THE CREATIVE IDENTITY of Austin, Texas, resident, Rob Lewis. A poet and digital artist, Lewis adopted the Stikmanz pseudonym during a period in which he regularly created abstract ambient video projections for trance parties, gallery shows and festival installations. The alternate identity has become a convenience for distinguishing his work from that of others named Rob Lewis active in creative fields. Author of three out of print chapbooks of poetry, this La Porte, Texas, native continues to develop graphic, video and literary projects. *Prelude to a Change of Mind* is his first novel. You can contact Rob by visiting his Web site: *www.robertstikmanz.com.*

*Photograph by J. X. Nye*